HER ALIEN STUDENT

STRANDED ON EARTH

BOOK THREE

IVY KNOX

Cover art: Natasha Snow Designs

Edited by: Tina's Editing Services, Chrisandra's Corrections, Mel Braxton Edits, & Owl Eyes Proofs & Edits

❀ Created with Vellum

AUTHOR'S NOTE

If you don't have any concerns regarding content and how it may affect you, **feel free to skip ahead to avoid spoilers**!

This book contains scenes that reference or depict sexual harassment, memories of domestic violence, rape mention, custody battle, police abusing their power, narcissism, systemic racism, as well as graphic violence which may be triggering for some. If you or someone you know is in need of support, there are places you can go for help. I have listed some resources at the end of this book.

CHAPTER 1

ZEVSSANAI "ZEV"

When I devised this plan, I wasn't expecting to feel so sticky. Yet here I sit, with my back fused to a chair that's far too small to hold my frame, beads of sweat soaking my hairline, my slick palms leaving wet marks on my pants as I wipe them off. If I stood right now, a puddle would occupy the space where my ass used to be.

Does this music room not have air conditioning? Does this school not have chairs fit for post-pubescent humans?

As my eyes scan the room, I don't notice anyone else struggling with excessive perspiration. Though, to be fair, it is late September in New Hampshire, and the temperatures are finally starting to drop. Everyone in the classroom is wearing long sleeves, and a few of them even entered the room wearing light jackets. It must just be me.

For that, I blame Charlie.

Charlie and her wide, toothy smile, her intricate blonde braids that reach the middle of her back, her thick thighs and even thicker tummy that jiggles when she moves. I have dreamed of that jiggle several times. I've had the typical fantasies of her kissing me, of course, of her sucking my cock and massaging my balls just the way I like and her riding me until my come fills her hot, swollen cunt. But none of those images are as deeply rooted in my brain as that subtle movement of flesh is. How does such a minuscule detail occupy so many of my waking hours?

Because she is soft and radiant. Ours, my draxilio purrs. *She is perfection incarnate.*

He'll get no argument from me. I have known for some time that Charlie is the one I'm meant to spend my life with. Since he and I are aligned on this, I'm not sure why my eyes haven't turned red. That's the sign that the two parts of me—my flightless form and my draxilio form—agree that we've found what the humans refer to as "the one." At least it was for my brothers Luka, Axil, and Mylo anyway. But not me. Not yet.

It will happen, my draxilio vows.

I don't share his confidence.

I may have been birthed in the same pod as my brothers, but to our handlers and the rest of the population on Sufoi, we are mutants. Genetically modified draxilios created for only one purpose: to serve the king by destroying anyone who threatens his rule. Taking a mate wasn't supposed to be possible for any of us.

After we crashed on Earth and began to commingle with humans, Luka, Kyan, and I began to show signs of having unique powers. Axil and Mylo, however, don't seem to contain the same kind of abilities. Perhaps it's the same with love. Some of us react a certain way upon discovering our mate—the whites of our eyes turning blood red—while the rest of us just...know.

Or perhaps the longer we spend trying to blend in with humans, the more our bodies acclimate to the human experience. It's not as if humans have a biological reaction to meeting the person they wish to marry. They feel the rightness of it, and they chase that feeling.

The deep corners of my mind where the trauma of my youth is carefully stored would argue that neither theory is true. That I stand alone in my inherent wrongness. That my brothers are the results of innovative and intentional genetic alterations that make them stronger and smarter, and I am merely the runt of the litter.

"Hi, everyone," Charlie says excitedly as she enters the classroom.

She takes a moment to get settled, then takes a seat in the center of the room. "My name is Charlotte Brooks, but y'all can just call me Charlie, and we're going to learn the basics of how to play guitar."

She pushes her teal glasses up the slender bridge of her nose as she props her guitar on her thigh and tosses her blonde braids over her shoulder, sending a thick cloud of her intoxicating scent in my direction. Closing my eyes, I inhale deeply, and it eases some of the tension in my shoulders. It's a warm yet spicy fragrance that reminds me of cinnamon and freshly picked apples.

Charlie must not find out I'm an exceptional guitar player. Then there would be no reason for me to take her class. I'm prepared to play the fool so I may spend an hour with her once a week for the next three months. It may seem like a silly ruse to some, or even a "complete waste of time," as Kyan put it, when I could simply tell Charlie that her laugh melts my bones and the curve of her plump pink lips sets my skin ablaze.

"Just ask her if she'll have dinner with you," Kyan offered this morning over coffee after he mercilessly mocked my plan to attend her class.

"What if she says no?" I asked, my mind taking me back to the handful of times I attempted to flirt with women over the years, and how poorly each encounter went. "You know I'm not a skilled conversationalist. People think I'm odd."

To this, Kyan merely replied, "Then fuck her," which was not helpful in the least. He's protective of me, and while I appreciate it, it does me no good in terms of wooing my mate.

I wish I could be as charming as Mylo. He makes flirting look effortless. Even Axil's quiet gruffness would be far more appealing than my inability to exchange pleasantries with people. When I try to flirt, my tongue feels as if it doubles in size, and I end up saying something that causes the woman to make up a flimsy excuse as to why she must leave immediately—the most common being that she left her faucet running at home. I'm certain it's a fabrication. It must be. Otherwise, there would be an extraordinary amount of water being wasted by the women of Earth.

No, being completely myself will not work with Charlie. I must be someone else. A man who is eager to learn how to play guitar, not an alien who has the ability to communicate with machines. When Charlie asks the class a question, I need to play dumb. I'm no thespian, but acting like a fumbling novice with my guitar shouldn't prove too difficult.

Softly, she strums her old Martin D-28, waking it up. The low, satisfied hum of her instrument meets my ears, a clear indication that she treats it well and knows precisely how to use it.

No one else can hear the instrument's voice but me. This power of mine is a gift and a curse at times, but with musical instruments, it feels like a gift.

Her guitar is covered in stickers, some faded and peeling, and I squint to see the names of her favorite bands. I can't make out many of them, but I make it a personal goal to learn each one.

"Before we get started, let's go around the room and have everyone share your name and a song that sparked your interest in learning guitar. How about we start over here?" She points to an older man on the left side of the room, and he coughs several times before speaking.

I don't listen to the responses of my classmates. It is not information I care to retain.

Instead, I focus on my teacher and learn the many expressions that light up her beautiful face. She is encouraging and engaged with each of her students' responses, showing them why choosing her class was the right decision. Upon hearing one young man's song choice, her hand covers her heart as she says, "Oh man, that solo had such a massive influence on me. When it gets to the dow-dinga-dinga-dow part in the middle," she shakes her head with her eyes closed, moved by the memory, "I felt it down to my toes. I swear to god."

The young man perks up in his seat, his posture transforming from casual to genuine excitement as he agrees with Charlie, and they continue to mimic the melody for another moment. It's clear that she's made him feel seen and valued. That's a power far more impactful than anything my brothers or I possess.

"And how about..." Charlie says, her gaze meeting mine for the first time, her smile growing so wide I can practically count her teeth. "Zev! Hey, good to see you." She seems surprised by my presence here, but there's something in her eyes that makes my heart flutter. Perhaps she's pleased to have me as a student? "Okay, well, you're up next."

Shit.

"Uh, hi," I mumble to the rest of the class, my voice slightly hoarse. "I'm Zev." *That's the easy bit, genius. Now you have to share a song that inspired you.*

I should've been trying to come up with an answer while my classmates were sharing theirs. What if I pick one that's already been said? What if Charlie thinks the one I choose is boring and predictable? Why the fuck wasn't I paying attention? This is my first opportunity to impress her, and here I am, soaked in sweat, looking like an asshole.

I can't say "November Rain" or "Stairway to Heaven." Those are too obvious. "Free Bird" and "All Along the Watchtower" are also repeatedly praised in the world of guitar, so those are out. "Purple Rain" is unmatched, but everyone loves Prince. It's hardly a unique choice.

Although...these are timeless hits for a reason. Why am I trying to find some obscure answer that she might not even be familiar with?

"Zev?" Charlie asks, looking at me expectantly. "Do you want to share a song that inspired you to learn guitar?"

Just as I go to say pass and admit defeat, it comes to me. "'From the Edge of the Deep Green Sea,' by The Cure," I say, rushing to get the words out before I stumble over them.

Charlie's brow lifts as she nods. "Wow, I love that answer," she says, turning to the rest of the class. "I didn't expect to hear that one today, but Porl Thompson, the guitarist, really enhanced the emotional intensity of it with that solo. Solid pick, Zev," she says proudly before moving to the student behind me.

She sees us too, my draxilio points out. *Patience.*

A deep breath whooshes out of my lungs. My body suddenly feels two tons lighter and significantly less damp.

"All right, let's get into it," Charlie begins. But I'm not ready to move on yet.

"Wait," I call out, way louder than is necessary, "what is your song?"

She jerks back slightly. "My song?"

"The song that inspired you to learn guitar."

Charlie's head drops, and her cheeks darken. "'Iris' by The Goo Goo Dolls."

It's not a song I know, but one I intend to learn the second I get home. *"Iris" by The Goo Goo Dolls. "Iris" by The Goo Goo Dolls.*

"That song was a big part of my high school experience," she explains. "You won't see it on any top ten lists, but whenever I hear those opening notes, I get chills. It's the first song that really made me feel alive, you know? Like I wasn't alone." She bites her lip as her gaze drops to the floor. "The moment I picked up a guitar, I knew that if just hearing the song felt like a balm to my soul, playing it would be even sweeter."

"Great song," the coughing man says with a smile.

For the briefest of moments, I'm envious of that man. That he's the one sharing this moment with Charlie and not me.

Calm yourself, my draxilio chides. *This will be remedied soon enough.*

I'm not entirely comfortable with him being the voice of reason when he's usually the part of me I need to talk down.

After the sharing portion of the class is over, Charlie starts going through the basic elements of the guitar, the chords and the position of our hands in order to play those chords, how to hold the pick, and how to navigate between the strings and frets. She goes through the proper positioning a few times before asking the rest of us to give it a try. Then she has to stop to fix a few guitars that are clearly out of tune.

As she works with students one on one, the woman next to me leans over and asks, "Is this how she wants us to hold it?"

She's a woman in her late sixties, most likely, with a kind smile, a light blue sweatshirt with a cartoon pig on it, and glasses thicker than an ice cream sandwich. Perhaps my fond memories of the late Lady

Norton compel me to offer my assistance, or maybe it's because I admire this woman's drive to develop a new skill later in life. Either way, I make sure Charlie is busy with another student before adjusting the woman's fingers to the proper position.

"You want to make sure you're pressing on the strings with just the tips of your fingers," I explain, "not flat. Otherwise, it won't sound right."

"Oh, okay," she says, trying it herself. It still doesn't sound right, and her guitar is practically screaming at her to remain on the tips of her fingers.

Only I can hear the guitar's pitiful pleas, and I do my best to ignore them.

Shortly after my brothers and I landed on Earth, I discovered my ability to communicate with machines and other mechanical devices. I'm not sure how or why I was gifted with this power, but anything from a small padlock to the power grid of New York City sings to me, as if I am the only one who can operate them properly. They don't speak using words, but the sounds they make indicate how they feel and what they seek.

Picking locks was how I first tested my newfound power, and I would follow the hums and groans the locks would emit until they popped open. Every device that followed spoke to me the same way. They can feel my intentions, and they are eager to help me get what I want.

Because of this power, learning how to play instruments is exceptionally easy, and though I have mastered the violin, the piano, and the flute, I know I will never run out of songs to play, and that's how I wish to spend my time. Recently, I quit my job as a tattoo artist to pursue this musical path.

"Your fingers are still a bit too flat," I tell the older woman, picking up my guitar so she can copy what I do. "You want to anchor your pointer finger here. When you stay on the tips of your fingers, it'll be easier to slide from one chord to the next. Like this…" I quickly show her the transition from E major to A major. "Strum, pick each string, then strum again."

"Well, well, well," Charlie says, standing mere inches to my left. "Looks like somebody should be in the advanced class."

I jump at the closeness of her, and the words fall from my lips before I can stop them. "No. No, no, no. It was just a lucky guess. I don't know anything." A hard lump forms in my throat, and I struggle to choke it down. "I'm an idiot like her," I say, pointing to the woman I was just helping. "Like everyone else here. Wh-why else would we be here?"

My draxilio sighs in disappointment. *Well, it doesn't get much worse than that.*

CHAPTER 2

CHARLOTTE "CHARLIE"

The drive home from Sudbury Elementary is short, and I spend the entirety of it replaying tonight's class in my head. It went well for the most part. The students seemed excited to learn, and I'm looking forward to getting to know each of them better. I've taught this class seven times in two different cities, and the first day always tends to be hit or miss. People are shy and don't see their own potential yet, so awkward moments are a given.

Then there's Zev. He takes awkward to another level. I feel for the guy. In the few interactions we've had prior to tonight, he's been nervous. Blunt. It's almost as if he has no filter and wishes he could step out of his own skin.

Maybe he's been bullied in the past. That would certainly explain it. Though I don't see how anyone could look at Zev and feel compelled to mock him. The man is gorgeous in an edgy sort of way. He wears black leather and ripped T-shirts and has tattoos running from knuckles to neck. If I met him during high school, my dad would've warned me to stay the hell away from him. "That boy is nothing but trouble," he would've said. The kind of man you'd picture running a motorcycle club if he weren't so visibly uncomfortable at being the center of attention.

I don't know why he's taking my class. He clearly knows more than he's letting on. If I hadn't overheard him telling Mrs. Elridge where to place her fingers, the guilty look on his face when I caught him was proof enough that he's not a novice. So why bother paying the two hundred dollars and showing up to learn a skill he already knows? It's baffling.

Maybe I read the situation wrong. After he insulted the entire class, he apologized profusely and struggled with the chord changes as we strummed along as a group. Was it for show? Perhaps my comment wounded his pride and messed up his rhythm. I meant it as a compliment. He seemed like he had already mastered the basics. I should be more careful next time and not make assumptions about the skill level of my students.

The other thing that was impossible not to notice was the way he looked at me. It wasn't the same focused attention I received from the rest of the class. This was different. More. His gaze was so intense, I wondered if he could see through my pores. Not in a scrutinizing way. It was like he was trying to learn me, memorize my features as if he was about to lose his sight and didn't want to forget a single detail.

Not that I mind. It's been years since a man has looked at me like that, and I've never received that kind of attention from someone as hot as Zev. I was practically squirming in my seat as he watched me. I felt the blood rush to my cheeks and never leave. Is it even physically possible to blush for sixty minutes straight? Before tonight, I would've said no. Hopefully the rest of my students didn't notice.

"Heyy, family," I sing-shout as I close the front door behind me.

"In the kitchen," my dad hollers over the sound of a sizzling pan.

Dad bought this small American craftsman about eight years ago. After spending two decades as a branch manager for a bank in Nashua, he retired as soon as he was old enough to collect benefits. He didn't hate the job; he just didn't want to do it anymore, and because of his frugal lifestyle, he was able to enter retirement comfortably.

The house is sparsely decorated in the way you'd expect a single man's home would be. He has just enough furniture to meet his needs, enough shelf space to hold his books and old DVDs, and nothing more.

I had to convince him to buy a loveseat so Nia and I had a place to sit in the living room. Until then, all he had was his black leather recliner. There aren't any knickknacks on the mantel above the fireplace, no candles on the coffee tables, no art on the walls apart from large, framed photos of Nia, Dad, and me together and Mom and Dad when she was still alive.

She's been gone for thirty years, but her face is in every room of this house. I don't remember her at all, but Dad has always made it a priority for her presence to be felt. I appreciate that about him.

"Mommy! Mommy! Mommy!" Nia shouts as she charges toward me.

I drop my guitar case, my purse, and my tote bag on the floor of the living room and open my arms wide as she rushes into them. "Baby!" I cry out with matching zeal. "What's up, princess? You being good for Grandpa tonight?"

She shakes her head no and swings the rest of her body with it.

"Uh-oh, what's going on?"

My father lets out an exaggerated groan as he leans against the kitchen doorway. "Well, let's see." He looks down at his fingers as he begins the tally of offenses.

I gasp playfully as I look at her. "There's a whole list? That's a bad sign."

"She won't stop messing with her tooth. I keep telling her it'll come out when it's ready to come out and not a moment before, but she won't listen."

"Nia, the tooth fairy doesn't show up for pulled teeth and you know that." I crouch down to her side and tug her against me as I tickle her sides. She giggles and leans harder into my chest. "She is a businesswoman, baby. And her business is fallen-out teeth. Not pulled. You think she won't know the difference? This is what she does."

Dad nods. "Mmm-hmm. That's what I said. That's exactly what I said."

"I know you want to get paid," I tell her, "but you gotta be patient. You're only five. There's plenty of time to drop those baby teeth and start building your empire."

She ducks her chin and stares absently at her pink-striped socks. "You hear me?"

Nia nods with a not-so-subtle frown. "'Kay."

The girl is already so money hungry, I'm convinced she's going to have a successful career in finance. I just need to make sure she doesn't take a wrong turn into pyramid schemes or some shit.

Sighing, I rise to my feet and tuck her head against my hip. Her soft, puffy pigtail fills the inside of my palm. "Now, what else went down while I was teaching?"

I hear my dad "psh" under his breath as he turns and shuffles his slippered feet back into the kitchen to stir what smells like veggies and chicken in sesame oil. My stomach growls in response. His stir-fry is the best. "She keeps playing that song I hate." He grabs a wooden spoon and points it at me. "That's on you, not her. You're the one that introduced her to that White-boy music."

Nia follows on my heels as I head into the kitchen.

"Which song? I listen to a lot of White-boy music."

He answers without looking up from the pan. "You know the one. Sounds like he's trying to sing, but it's more like a whiny child."

That certainly narrows it down to the emo hits of the early aughts, but not by much.

"The dance, dance song," he says. "What do they call themselves? Grudge Guys?"

"You mean Fall Out Boy?" I correct him through a steady stream of laughter. He's very aware of how much I enjoy all genres and periods of music, but never misses a chance to needle me over songs from that particular time.

She starts singing "Dance, Dance" as she tilts her head back and spins in a tight circle.

I join in with the rest of the chorus, knowing my dad doesn't hate the song as much as he says. I've heard him humming it while shaving.

"You girls keep that up and I'm going to eat all this myself," he warns, lifting the pan off the stove and showing us the colorful assortment of red bell peppers, carrots, pea pods, baby corn, and chunks of chicken in between. "Put on Sade or Rema. I deserve peace while I eat."

Both artists are heavily featured on my Chill Vibes playlist, so I'm happy to comply. I pull up Spotify on my phone and play the best of Sade, her velvet voice filling the living room and kitchen through the Sonos speaker next to the TV. Another indulgence I forced upon him after suffering through too many of my favorite songs being played through shoddy, cheap speakers that die within an hour.

"I'm hungry," Nia whines as soon as she stops spinning. She sways a bit and starts to stumble, but I catch her before she can take a single faltering step.

"No spinning in the kitchen while Grandpa's cooking. Remember?" I tell her sternly. "We got hot pans and sharp knives. Here," I hand her three napkins. "Help me set the table." She sets them out in our regular spots while I grab everything else.

Dinner passes the way it usually does. Nia eats most of the food on her plate without complaint before politely asking if she can go turn on the TV. Dad gets a second helping of dinner and downs two cans of Pepsi, barely managing to talk himself out of a third. I don't typically get to enjoy my meal until Nia leaves the table, and by that time, it's lukewarm at best, but I eat every bite and usually the rest of hers too.

As I load the plates into the dishwasher, Dad sidles up to me with a glass of red wine in hand. "Things are going well with Joyce," he says, a warm smile playing on his lips.

"Oh yeah? Any big date plans this weekend?" I ask, rinsing the mushy bits of rice and carrots off Nia's plate.

He chuckles softly. "Not this weekend, but we were talking about moving in together sometime soon."

The warm water bathing my hands struggles to heat the chill now racing through my bones.

It's not that I don't like Joyce. I do. She's a sweet woman in her late fifties that my dad met at bingo. We've had dinner together a few times, the four of us, and she's been kind to me and Nia. They've been together about six months—much longer than any of his previous girl-friends have stuck around—and she makes him incredibly happy.

The panic that fills my chest is due to the direction this conversation is taking. Joyce lives in a two-bedroom apartment with her recently widowed sister. There's no way my dad's planning on moving there, so that means Joyce would move in here.

"I see," I mumble distantly as I drop a pod of dish detergent into the dishwasher. "How soon were you thinking?"

He sets his wine glass next to the sink and places a hand on my arm. "I'm not trying to kick you out of here. I want you to know that." Dad lets out a heavy sigh. "It might get a little crowded once she's here, is all. So take as long as you need to find a place. There's no set date she needs to be out of her apartment or anything like that. No rush."

I rinse the soap from my hands and dry them slowly as I let the information settle. My eyes focus intently on the bright blue dish towel in my hands. It's covered in dragons—Nia's favorite thing in the world—she picked it out at Target last weekend the moment she saw it.

Part of me wants to be mad at him. I'm inclined to shout, "What the hell am I supposed to do? Where do you expect us to live?" But Dad deserves to embrace the love he's found and really see where it goes. This might be the woman who takes care of him for the rest of his days. I can't deny him that even if it's a million times more convenient for me. Besides, it's time for Nia and me to have our own place. Dad converted a small office into her room before we moved in, and she and I currently share a bathroom, which hasn't been ideal.

He's let me rebuild my credit by allowing us to live here rent free these last few months. I knew that wasn't going to last forever, nor did I want it to.

"That's great, Dad," I finally tell him, dropping the towel and giving his hand a gentle squeeze. "Take the leap. I'm proud of you."

He levels me with a serious look, the lines of his forehead deepening. "I'm serious, now. There's no rush, you hear me?"

"I hear you."

I follow him into the living room, and we settle into our seats, him in his recliner with the remote resting on his stomach, me stretched out on the loveseat, and Nia on the floor playing with the pink stuffed dragon toy she calls "Otto" that Joyce gifted her last time she was here. Dad nods off to an old episode of *CSI: Miami* as I try to wrap my head around moving.

I haven't had my name on a lease in years, and I wasn't ready to do it again this soon. I've just been crashing with friends and family in various cities, hoping to stay off the grid. Applying for an apartment means putting down roots. It means hard inquiries on my credit score. It's a paper trail anyone can use to find me. That *he* can use to find me. And I need to stay hidden.

CHAPTER 3

ZEV

"*I* listened to The Goo Goo Dolls," I tell Charlie the moment class ends. It's been seven days since I last saw her, and for all seven days, I have listened to "Iris" on repeat. I've learned it on guitar and piano. It's a hauntingly beautiful song, and I wish more than anything I could play it for her. But I can't. Not yet.

Charlie thinks I'm a novice, and that's how it must remain.

"Yeah?" she asks as she closes her guitar case. Her cheeks darken and her gaze evades mine. "What'd you think?"

Is she worried I've judged her taste in music? Could my opinion mean that much to her?

"I loved it," I tell her honestly. "I listened to the entire album and the rest of their catalog. Their original sound was much more punk, but with the release of the song 'Name' in September 1995, they cemented their signature alternative/pop sound. It's a shame the original guitarist left the band before they reached peak fame, but I like that John and Robby have remained a steadfast duo."

Her eyes widen as she stills, and my heart makes a frenzied thump as I wonder if I said something incorrect.

Eventually, she smiles. "Spent some time on Wikipedia, did you?"

"Yes," is all I say because I can't tell if she's impressed or embarrassed on my behalf. I thought knowing everything about the band behind her favorite song would, I don't know, dazzle her. Show that I care. Perhaps I misread the situation.

She crosses her arms over her chest and tilts her head slightly, her gaze hot as it travels down my body. The scrutiny causes me to shift on my feet.

"What's your second favorite song by them?"

I don't know why, but this feels like it could be a trick. Charlie is testing me. This is not where I excel in the human world. These little games they play with one another, waiting to see if someone falls into a verbal trap of their own making—I find it vexing. Why can't humans simply say what they mean?

Honestly is the only way I know how to communicate. Anything else is too much effort. "'Black Balloon,'" I tell her. "It has the same dreamlike feeling as 'Iris,' but the lyrics make no sense. Though it is lovely, I have no idea what the song means."

Charlie laughs, and it's a mouth-wide-open, delightfully jovial laugh that tells me it's real. "I don't know what it means either. Never have. I went to one of their shows a few years ago and when 'Black Balloon' came on, people in the crowd started tossing out all these black balloons, and it was such a…such a moment, you know? We were batting them around like beach balls for the rest of the night."

The words slip out before I can stop them. "What's a beach ball?"

She jerks back, and her brow furrows. "Seriously?"

"No," I begin, shaking my head and plastering on a self-depre-cating smirk, "not seriously. I know what a beach ball is." I clear my throat, trying to appear nonchalant. "Obviously."

Charlie doesn't look like she buys it, but she also doesn't push me on it, for which I am thankful.

It must be exactly what it sounds like, my draxilio offers. *A ball filled with beach sand. Or a ball the same color as the beach.*

Neither of those sound correct. *Tonight, we Google,* I send back.

"What about other songs?" she asks, changing the subject. "Songs you like or that make you happy, but you don't know what they mean?"

My answer comes easily. "'Come On Eileen.'" I throw my hands up. "It's a charming song that always sticks in my head, but the lyrics are baffling."

"I can see that," she replies. "The whole *too-ra-lu-ra* part feels like it's supposed to be a pickup line, but if it is, it's a terrible one."

I nod emphatically, pleased by the common ground we've established. "Precisely."

We walk out to the parking lot together as she continues our discussion. "I think 'Call Me Maybe' is my happy, silly song. I love it, but how can you miss someone before they come into your life? Not knocking on Carly, but, girl, what?"

I've heard the song Charlie speaks of, and those lyrics never confused me. "It's the longing for that someone meant for you whom you have yet to find, and when you do discover them, it's hard not to think about the time you spent apart. All that time wasted when you could've been together..."

Charlie's eyes are locked on mine, intensity and heat swirling in her copper irises. "Guess I never thought of it like that."

"Allow me," I say, taking her guitar case from her hands and putting it in her open trunk. Her expression remains a combination of thankfulness and surprise when I open the driver's side door for her.

"Are you, um," Charlie stammers as she climbs into her car, "are you going to Twilight night at the library tomorrow?"

Mylo has been encouraging me to attend this event for weeks, and I have continued to refuse, but now that Charlie's asking... "Of course. I wouldn't miss it."

"Great." She puts her keys in the ignition but keeps one foot on the ground as if reluctant to end our chat. "Well, I'll see you then. You're dressing up, right?"

"Right," I reply instantly.

"Okay. Night, Zev."

She pulls her car door shut, and I watch as she drives off into the night.

When I arrive home, my brothers and their mates are in the kitchen and arguing loudly.

"Why are you in such a foul mood this evening?" my brother Mylo asks my brother Kyan, who is slamming each cabinet door he opens as he searches for something.

"Well, *brother*," Kyan utters the word as if it burns his tongue. "My COO hired an assistant for me because she says I've been taking on too much, and when I carry this stress around, it's a bad look for the company, or some such nonsense."

I ignore all of them as I head straight for the TV.

"Okay, well, she's right," Sam, Mylo's mate, says with a shrug.

Kyan looks aghast. "I have not even met this woman! Thea said she's qualified and interviewed well, but that means nothing to me. I should be the one vetting candidates for this position. Not that this role is even necessary. I'm perfectly capable of running the company without anyone's help."

Vanessa, my brother Axil's mate, rubs her growing belly as she shakes her head at Kyan. "Kyan dear, I adore you, but Thea made the right call."

Sam pops a sweet-potato chip in her mouth and mutters, "Yeah, give that woman a raise."

"You look like you haven't slept in weeks," Vanessa continues. "Having an assistant will take some of the day-to-day bullshit off your plate."

"Where can I find the *Twilight* films?" I ask without turning around. All these streaming channels, and I can never find what I'm looking for.

Sam perks up at that. "Ooh, are we marathoning for trivia night tomorrow?" she asks, hopping out of her seat and coming to join me in the living room. "I'm down. I haven't seen *Eclipse* in a minute."

"You're going?" Mylo asks, his arms crossed over his chest. "You said you were a no."

"Yes, well, I've changed my mind," I explain.

Vanessa comes over and sits in the big leather chair and guides me to the Prime Video app, showing me where her purchased movies are.

"Now I need to figure out which of these characters I'm going to dress as."

Axil grunts as he leans his forearms on the back of Vanessa's chair. "This is because of Charlie, isn't it?"

"You should be James or one of the Volturi. Aro, probably," Sam babbles, presumably to me, but also to herself. "You have the perfect hair for Aro."

"The villains?" Vanessa scoffs. "Charlie Swan is the one you should dress up as. That man is a full zaddy."

Sam groans loudly. "The cop? The fucking cop? No. That's not going to score any points with Charlie." She turns to Vanessa. "And the one true zaddy is Pedro Pascal. Everyone else is like a zaddy in training."

Kyan swallows half a bottle of water in one gulp and looks questioningly between the two women. "Do you know what they're saying?" he asks Mylo and Axil. "Because I require translation."

"Don't worry about it," Sam says, waving her hand dismissively. "You should get some sleep, Ky. Big day tomorrow with your new assistant, right?"

Kyan growls as he stomps up the steps toward his wing of the house.

"If we're all going to watch these films, I need it to be quiet," I tell them. "I must pay attention."

Axil urges Vanessa to go with him back to their house next door so she may get some sleep. Sam and Mylo stay with me through the first one and *New Moon*, but Sam nods off during *Eclipse*, and Mylo carries her to their bedroom. It won't be their bedroom much longer as they've purchased the house on the other side of ours. Slowly, the Monroes seem to be acquiring the entire street.

I stay up until the credits of *Breaking Dawn: Part Two* begin to roll as the sun makes its climb into the sky. Exhausted, I carry myself down the hall toward my room and manage to kick my pants off before I flop onto the bed. This day will be a waste, but at least I know what my costume for tonight will be.

* * *

"Wow," Sam says as she hands me a cup of fruit punch. Her normally curly brown hair is straight tonight, with a thin black headband holding it off her face. She wears a fitted royal blue dress that's torn at her left thigh, and black heels. Though her skin is much darker than the sickly pale of the Cullens, Sam's cheeks and nose sparkle softly in the light, and her lips are a deep crimson. A perfect Bella. "Emmett Cullen, huh?"

I self-consciously run a hand over my overly gelled hair and adjust the socks balled up beneath my sleeves. "Don't I look like him?" Emmett is buff, with milky white skin and short hair. Those were his three most defining physical features, so that's what I focused on when assembling this look.

"You do, but you don't need the bicep pads, Zev," Sam notes, poking at the sock against my arm. "You're already jacked."

"No, I am not," I tell her. Being leaner than the rest of my brothers, my muscles are not as prominent as Axil's or even Luka's. I don't appear wafer thin, but I'm certainly not as beefy as Emmett Cullen, so the socks seemed necessary.

"Whatever," she mutters before taking a sip of punch. "I'm going to find my Edward." She nods toward the drink table. "Charlie's over there. I think you'll like her costume. Amazing you two didn't plan this."

My eyes scan past the milling crowd of people with their red and gold contacts, brown and blond wigs, their fake fangs, and drab, functional attire that perfectly suits the Pacific Northwest climate as much as it fits New Hampshire in early fall. My mouth drops open the moment I spot Charlie.

Dressed in a low-cut, fitted gray blazer, loosely draped white scarf, dark jeans that fit her like a second skin, gray heels, and a blonde wig hanging in loose waves around her shoulders, Charlie glows like the only source of light in a dark room. Her red eyes match her mouth, and when she smiles, her pointy fangs hang over her plump bottom lip. A lip I would very much like to suck on.

"Rosalie," I say, slightly breathless at the sight of her, and the knowledge that in the world of *Twilight*, she is my better half. My angel.

"No fucking way," Charlie says, her hand going to cover her mouth as she takes me in. "How did you know?"

"I didn't. Emmett is my favorite Cullen," I explain. "He seems to consistently have the most fun. Doesn't take himself too seriously."

She nods. "Fair point."

"You are the consummate Rosalie."

She giggles as she gives me a twirl. "I like her backstory the best."

"Ah, yes. As I recall, she killed her ex-fiancé and the pack of atrocious men who violated her. Do you also have villains from your past that need to be crushed?"

Briefly, so briefly I almost don't catch it, her face hardens and a flicker of rage dances in her eyes. "Pretty sure every woman does."

As much as I'm desperate for more information—like the names and addresses of Charlie's foes—I decide to change the subject. "How's the event going?"

"Good," she says proudly. "We had so many people participating in the trivia portion that we had to have it out here instead of in the conference room. And these folks know their stuff. It came down to a lightning round. The Forkable Bellas ended up winning. They're right over there."

She points to a group of women of various sizes and ages dressed as Bella. Most of them are dressed as innocent, pre-vampire Bella with her utility jackets, but a few of them opted for the confident, immortal Bella with drops of fake blood splattered across their sleeker Cullen-money outfits.

"Looking sharp, brother," Mylo says as he strolls up to us with Sam on his arm. His light brown hair is mussed and high as Edward Cullen. He left the glasses he doesn't need at home, and wears a tight, button-up blue shirt, the sleeves rolled up, with a black leather cuff around his wrist.

"Same to you," I reply.

Sam stares up at him dreamily, and they share a deeply passionate kiss. Charlie averts her eyes, looking distinctly uncomfortable. I would feel the same if I wasn't so used to their public displays of affection. They cannot keep their hands off each other.

When the kiss ends, Sam jerks back to give Charlie a strange look. "I thought you were dressing up as Alice."

Charlie lifts her shoulder in a half-shrug. "I mean, she's weird in a fun way, but Rosalie's vengeance is more my vibe."

"Hey, guys," a female voice calls from behind us.

"For fuck's sake," Sam groans quietly. When the woman approaches us, Sam's smile tightens. "Caitlyn. What are you doing here?"

Caitlyn. The name is familiar, but I'm not sure why.

Caitlyn shoves her hands into the pockets of her black jeans. "Just a lonely vampiress looking for her Carlisle. Seen any blood-sucking doctors around here that I can chat up?"

Ah, she is dressed as Esme.

Mylo scratches his chin. "I'm afraid the crowd tonight is mostly women."

"Aren't you married?" Sam blurts, staring daggers at the short woman over her cup of punch. "And where's Beth? I'll be honest, if you brought her here, I might have to take a wooden stake and–"

"Caitlyn, is it?" Mylo interrupts. "The drinks are over there, and we also have meat and vegetarian sliders from Burgatory. They're delicious. You should try them."

So this is the petite sidekick of Beth, Vanessa and Sam's arch-nemesis from their days in school. I understand Sam's heated glare now.

Mylo takes Sam's hand and tries to guide her away before the conversation takes a tumultuous turn, but Caitlyn is eager to reply, "I'm divorced now. Thank the good Lord. Also, Beth isn't here. We're kind of on the outs, I guess. She's a dick."

"Here, here!" Sam shouts, lifting her red cup.

Mylo whispers something into her ear as he pulls her away, toward the group of kids waiting at the front desk. I expect Caitlyn to leave once it's just the three of us, but she remains. "Emmett and Rosalie, eh?" she says, looking between Charlie and me.

"Yep," Charlie replies. Her tone is somewhat clipped, but I don't think Caitlyn notices.

Caitlyn nods. "You guys are cute. I'm Caitlyn, by the way. Divorced, Beth's former friend. Just in case you didn't catch that."

Charlie laughs as she shakes Caitlyn's hand. Caitlyn's self-awareness seems to disarm my mate enough for introductions to be made. "Charlie. Pleasure."

"I'm also the town clerk, mother of two boys who now call me by my first name, and painfully single. So, you know, if you know anyone…" she looks me up and down. "That includes you too, big boy. If you guys aren't a thing, of course."

"Um," I mumble uncomfortably. "No thank you."

Caitlyn shrugs. "That's cool. Offer stands."

"Wow," Charlie says as Caitlyn saunters off. "She is something."

I try to shake off the interaction. "Something I do not want near me." It's not that female attention is foreign to me. When you're over seven feet tall, the women of Earth take notice. While I appreciate that anyone finds my physical form appealing, it's not my true form. It's a mask. If they were to see me in my true form with the horns and blue scales, or my draxilio form, the reaction would be quite different.

There was a time when female attention was something I sought out, but since finding Charlie, I'd prefer to be invisible to everyone but her. Her gaze is the only one I want.

"I was thinking about you today," Charlie says as her hand rests lightly on my forearm, causing my stomach to flip.

"Oh?"

She nods as she pushes her teal cat-eye glasses up her nose. "I was listening to Tyler, The Creator, and his song 'Garden Shed' has a solid guitar riff that I thought you'd appreciate."

Charlie thought of me. Not when I was sitting in front of her in class. Not when I was spouting a stream of facts by her car. She actually thought of me, unprompted, when we weren't in the same space.

That's a good sign, my draxilio purrs. *Do not lose this momentum.*

Right. I need to keep her engaged. See where this goes. "You should've texted me." Does she even have my number?

"I would've if I had your number," she replies with a smirk.

That answers that.

"I slid into your DMs instead."

I've heard of this, but I'm not entirely sure what it means.

"Check your Instagram. I requested to follow you too."

"My Instagram?" I ask, not remembering the last time I even opened the app on my phone.

Charlie grabs two cups of punch off the drink table and hands me one. "You don't use it?"

"I made the account when I worked for Tilton Tattoo. They said it was a requirement so clients could see my style and portfolio before booking with me. I set up the account and I quit that job not long after, so I made the account private. I haven't been on there much since."

"I get it. My account is private too," she says, looking distantly toward the door. "Don't need strangers knowing my business."

"I'll get back on it now that I know you're there," I tell her.

She fidgets with the sleeve of her blazer as she smiles, the skin around her eyes crinkling with mirth.

I don't understand why she seems surprised that I want to know more about her or spend more time talking to her. It's as if she hasn't been on the receiving end of genuine interest, which can't be the case. She's a spectacularly beautiful woman with a brilliant mind. Who wouldn't want to spend every remaining minute they have in this life talking to her?

"I thought of you too," I tell her. *Every second of every day since we met.* "The guitar solo in 'Don't Fear the Reaper' blew me away. I just...wanted to tell you that."

"Ah, such a good one," she says before noticing the line at the front desk. "Excuse me a sec." She steps away to speak with attendees and issue library cards. I don't mingle like she does, mostly because it's not my job, but also because I don't want to. Instead, I pick up empty plates and cups I find around the lobby and throw them into the trash receptacle, keeping my head down as I wander to avoid further interactions, particularly with Caitlyn.

The guests filter out slowly, and as the caterers clean up their station, Sam asks if I'd like to join them at Tipsy's for a nightcap. "Uh, I'm not sure."

She boos in frustration. "Charlie, you in?" she shouts across the room.

"Oh, no. I need to head home and check on the kiddo. Have fun though."

Sam turns back to me with a knowing glance. "You're out too then, I guess?"

"Afraid so."

If Charlie won't be in attendance, there's no reason for me to go.

The four of us say our goodbyes as Mylo locks the library doors, and as soon as I get home, I rinse the gel out of my hair and the sparkles from my skin and spend the next several minutes trying to remember my Instagram password. Eventually, I give up and reset it, and once I'm in, I find Charlie's message with a link to "Garden Shed."

My chest bones barely contain the exuberant thump of my heart as I read the message, "Thought of you when I heard this," and reread it again several times.

This leads me down a rabbit hole of hip-hop classics, as well as hits of today that I find particularly impressive. I end up sending her my favorite Outkast song, "B.O.B."

Once the message is sent, and the request to follow is returned, I wait patiently for her reply. The world fades away with my phone tucked against my chest.

CHAPTER 4

CHARLIE

This is not my fucking day. I thought it was when I woke up and discovered a DM from Zev, but then Nia ran into my room crying about wetting the bed, and things have gotten progressively shitty ever since.

Dad was already out of the house, over at Joyce's place for breakfast, I assume, so I ran around trying to clean up the mess as quickly as possible. Nia was cranky after a bad night of sleep and refused to eat her breakfast, so that took forever. It was a hostile negotiation that ended with her taking four bites of toast as long as I let her go to school wearing her favorite dragon pajamas.

By the time we make it out the door, we're already ten minutes late. The look on the teacher's face when I pull up to the curb is scathing. "I know, I'm so sorry," I say as I get out of the car.

"Come on, Nia," she says as Nia climbs down from her seat in the back.

I go to pull Nia in for a hug, and as she reaches for me, she knocks my mug loose from my grip, and coffee spills down the front of my dress. "Sh...sugar!" I shout, wishing I could let fly a series of expletives, but remembering just in time where the fuck I am. Luckily, the coffee has been sitting out long enough that it's no longer hot, but at this point, I don't have time to run home and change before work.

"Uh-oh," is all Nia says before chuckling and skipping off with her teacher.

"Shine bright, baby," I call out before the doors close behind her, though the words come out much grumpier than usual since I'm covered in coffee.

I show up at the library twenty minutes late for my shift, covered in coffee and completely frazzled. Before I can apologize to Mylo and beg him not to fire me, I notice the imposing silhouette of Councilman Grady Vincent, newly elected and recently charged with overseeing the library's book review.

"That's not good enough," Councilman Vincent says. "A list of titles isn't enough. I need summaries of each book to determine whether the content is suitable for the young readers of this town. Do you expect me to look up each book myself?"

"Yes, actually," Mylo replies. His tone is polite, but firm. "I was told a list of titles would be sufficient."

Is he seriously expecting Mylo to create a book report for each of the thousands of books we have in stock? The hell is wrong with this man?

"Who told you that?" the councilman barks back.

"Your assistant."

"Well, my assistant isn't the one who will be reviewing each book, are they?"

I highly doubt this prick is going to comb through all these books himself. Mylo shoots me a look that tells me he has the same thought, but, of course, that's not something either of us says aloud.

Quickly, I race into the back office and drop my coat and bag. As I step back into the lobby, I spot Officer Burton in the parking lot, standing directly behind my car. What's he doing? Why is he even here?

I've heard enough about him from Sam and Vanessa to know he's an evil, evil man. His nephew Trevor raped Vanessa in high school, and when she tried to report it, he pressured her into staying silent, pulling the same "but he has a promising future" bullshit so many women have to hear after the worst moment of their lives. A few years later, Trevor did the same to Sam, and knowing it was useless to pursue legal action, she stayed silent too. Who knows how many more women suffered because Officer Burton wanted to give his nephew a free pass to be violent?

He's also been harassing the Monroe brothers since Trevor died a few months ago. He blames Axil for Trevor's death, and I guess he assumes the rest of the boys helped Axil cover it up. I'm not sure why else a white cop would have such a vendetta against a group of chill white guys in their thirties.

He showed up here not long ago, interrupting a drag queen during story hour with the kids, accusing me and Mylo of exposing the innocent children of Sudbury to porn just because we had a gay romance displayed on the front table. The man is an absolute nightmare, and wherever he goes, pain follows.

"Shit," I grunt as I race outside. I think I know why he's scribbling on his little pad, but I'm really hoping I'm wrong.

"Officer Burton," I say through panting breaths once I reach the parking lot. "What, uh, what can I do for you?"

Be calm. Do what he says, I chant silently.

"Ms. Brooks, were you aware that your registration has expired?" he asks, ripping the ticket from his pad and shoving it into my hands.

This fucking day.

Should I play dumb and pretend I forgot? Or should I point out to this chapped-lipped potato-shaped bastard that it's only expired by four days? Four. Days. Does he really have nothing better to do than ride around and issue tickets to people covered in spilled coffee?

I look down at the ticket and my stomach sinks when I notice it's a hundred dollars. I just spent the last forty bucks in my checking account to pay for gas. My paycheck will hit the account in a few days, thank god, but most of it will go toward groceries, my student loans, and credit card balances. And, somehow, I'm supposed to find enough money to afford rent too?

"Um, respectfully, Officer Burton," I stammer, trying to keep my posture relaxed and my hands raised. He didn't ask me to raise them, but I'm keeping them raised. You never know what a cop will perceive as a threat. "Is there any way you could look the other way on this one? As soon as I get paid on Friday, I'll renew my registration online, I promise you."

"Look the other way?" he repeats with a sneer. "No, Ms. Brooks. I take my job very seriously, and if I always looked the other way, this town would be overrun with criminals."

Sure. As if this town isn't currently being patrolled by the shadiest motherfucker in the state. Whatever. It's not worth it.

"I understand," I tell him with a smile. Keeping my hands up, I walk backward toward the entrance. It isn't until I'm inside the safety of the building that I turn my back to him.

Mylo steps out from behind the desk and races toward me. "You okay? What did Burton want?"

I show him my ticket.

His frown turns into a deep scowl. "For what?"

"Registration. Expired on September thirtieth."

"As in…four days ago?" Mylo asks, incredulous.

"Yep. Oh, I'm sorry I was so late today, by the way. Nia was just–"

"Hey, no worries," he interjects. "It's fine." His gaze drops to the coffee covering the front of my light blue maxi shirt dress and he clicks his tongue. "Yeah, this is not your day."

I can't help but laugh. "It is not."

He steps behind the front desk and pulls a "Scholastic is Fantastic" shirt from a box and tosses it to me. "Feel free to rock the stain if you want, but if you prefer to cover it, throw that on. We had extra."

The T-shirt is a size too big, but I fold up the sleeves of my dress a few times and wrap the cloth belt of the dress around the middle of the T-shirt. It's not a particularly polished look, but at least now it looks somewhat intentional.

"Well, I need to head upstairs and begin preparing a detailed rundown of every book we have with their blurbs and trigger warnings," Mylo grumbles with a heavy sigh. "Even though I'd bet my life that the councilman will probably delete it the moment it hits his inbox."

It seems we're both stuck in a pile of bullshit today. "Good luck."

The rest of my shift passes without incident. It's a Thursday, so the library is pretty quiet, apart from a few of the regulars. One of those regulars is a homeless man I've seen here a bunch of times. He's an older Black gentleman and usually comes in near closing time to warm up or use the restroom. His mismatched sneakers are falling apart, and he wears a sweatshirt under two light jackets, one layered over the other. I think he might be a veteran. I recall seeing that written on the sign he holds up near the highway exit. We've never spoken, but he's quiet and keeps to himself.

Today he's reading the newspaper on a cushioned bench by the back windows, and as I approach him, he rushes to gather his few possessions. "I'm leaving. I'm leaving."

I've seen Officer Burton harassing him and throwing away his things, and I refuse to treat another human being with such blatant disrespect. "No, no. You don't have to leave," I assure him. "I'm just coming to introduce myself. I'm Charlie." I hold out my hand, and he stares at it for a full minute before taking it.

"Phil."

"Phil," I repeat. "You don't have to leave. We're open until six tonight. Stay as long as you want." As I let go of his hand, I lean in closer. "In fact, there's a bubbler and coffee station by the restrooms just down that hallway. It's kind of hidden and mostly used by staff but please help yourself."

His nose scrunches up as he tries to determine my motive or if I'm straight-up lying, but eventually, his eyes widen, and he offers a dozen thank-yous before heading toward the restrooms.

A few hours later, I pop my head into Mylo's office and say goodbye before I leave for the day, and he seems thankful for the break. "Guess I'll just have to resume this menial task tomorrow. What a tragedy."

"See you tomorrow, boss."

He offers me a gleeful salute, and I drive to Nia's school in a surprisingly good mood despite the way my day began.

Once dinner has been served, clean sheets put on Nia's bed, her teeth brushed, and her satin sleep bonnet donned, I change into my oversized TLC T-shirt and boxers and climb into bed.

I'm exhausted, but not too tired to open Instagram. Zev sent me "B.O.B" from Outkast, which is a truly excellent song, so I open Spotify to find the right one to send back.

> My day started off like this...

I begin with a link to "You're Standing on My Neck" by Honeyblood.

> But it ended up more like this...

I add, with a link to "Juice" by Lizzo.

The dots appear, and I stop breathing, eagerly awaiting his response as I clutch my phone so tightly, I'm surprised it doesn't crack right down the center.

> Zev: That sounds like a grim morning. I'm sorry to hear that. But I'm glad it didn't stay that way. 🥴

The woozy drunk face has me scratching my head.

> Sorry. Meant to send this one: 🙂

> LOL

> My day was mostly this...

He shares a link to "Look Who's Inside Again" by Bo Burnham, a song Burnham wrote during the pandemic about going stir-crazy inside, which sends me into a fit of laughter.

> But now that you're here, it's this…

It's a link to "Heat Wave" by Glass Animals, which has an unre-quited crush vibe to it.

Is he flirting with me?

> And this…

He sends a link to "Butterflies" by MAX and Ali Gatie.

Oh, he's definitely flirting with me. Is it okay that he's flirting with me though? He's technically my student. Since it's a once-a-week guitar class for adults, I doubt the rules are the same as they would be for a college professor dating a student, but still. I can't afford to lose that job, especially now that I have a one-hundred-dollar ticket to pay and future rent to factor in.

Still, I can't deny that flirting with Zev via song links is exactly how I wish to spend the rest of the night. I also can't deny the many fantasies I've had of him shirtless, playing "Iris" in my bedroom. Halfway through the song, he tosses the guitar to the floor because he's so distracted by the sight of me that he refuses to wait another second before devouring my pussy.

It's a very specific fantasy, and it gets me to the finish line without fail. Every. Single. Time.

But what am I supposed to say next? Flirting has never come natu-rally to me. I don't know how to be seductive. If my life depended on being sexy, I'd be dead in three seconds.

Zev doesn't seem to be good at it either, come to think of it. It felt like he was trying to flirt with me when he told me what he learned from The Goo Goo Dolls' Wikipedia page, but nothing about that exchange was sexy. It was adorable, of course, but not sexy. I kind of appreciate that about him though. He doesn't play games. He just tells the truth. I haven't met many men like that. Wasn't sure they even existed.

Fuck it. I'll take a page out of his book.

This is the best part of my day too.

I think I'm blushing. You're making me blush.

LOL you think? That's usually something you know.

Hard to know for sure. I can't see myself.

Hmm. I'm going to need proof. Selfie or you're lying.

Zev sends a photo of himself standing very close to his floor-length mirror. He's wearing loose navy-blue sweats and a faded gray Death Cab for Cutie T-shirt with a few small holes along his rib cage, and what look to be speckles of white paint along the bottom hem. He points to the pinkish hue found on his left cheek. His different-colored eyes are wide, and his expression is triumphant.

A loud cackle escapes me, and for a second, I worry it was loud enough to wake Nia. After a moment of quiet, I release the breath I was holding and zoom in on the pic from top to bottom. Not gonna lie, I wish the sweatpants were just a smidge tighter because these have no outline or bulge for me to drool over.

And those hands. Mm-mm-mm. His fingers are long and thick; the veins protruding across the backs of his hands have me squeezing my thighs together. I haven't had the opportunity to really focus on his hands during class, which is probably a good thing because watching those strong fingers strum those strings in the right order would probably leave me squirming in my seat.

Goddamn, this man is pretty.

Look at that. You are blushing.

I don't lie, Charlie.

That's good. I don't fuck with liars.

I pull up the photo again and zoom in on the reflection of his hand holding the phone as I slip my fingers beneath the waistband of my shorts. They glide easily through my slick folds, my clit hot and swollen as I picture his finger circling it instead of mine. I hear him whispering my name, the heat of his breath lifting the hair around my ear.

Chills race across my skin. My hips roll as I insert a finger, then a second, letting out a shuddering breath as my body desperately seeks the friction only his calloused fingers could deliver.

Pulling the nearest pillow against my face, I drop my phone onto the comforter and let the pillow absorb my cries of pleasure as I pump my hand in and out of my core. Keeping an eye on the photo, silently commanding the screen to not go dark, my pace turns erratic as I chase my release.

It seems you're meant to fuck with me then.

I explode as the words flash across my screen, the walls of my pussy contracting around my fingers.

If only he dropped the "with."

CHAPTER 5

ZEV

*C*harlie and I spent the rest of the week, and the weekend, sending each other songs over Instagram. Sometimes it was a song that captured our mood at the time, other times it was a song that reminded us of the other. I've gotten to know so much more about her just through the songs she listens to.

She seems to enjoy Bo Burnham's musical comedy as much as I do, which was a thrilling discovery.

The best part is that the songs have become a way to continue the conversation. We reach natural stopping points throughout our days, when one of us is busy, or when we fall asleep at night, but then she or I will drop back into the other's DMs with a song link, and it leads to another long chat. I've learned that she's allergic to shellfish, she broke her wrist twice in one year, she hates golf and loves basketball, she's terrified of snakes, and can speak German fluently.

Now, knowing these things about her, it's not weird or creepy of me to visit her at work. At least, I hope it isn't. I spent the entirety of my Sunday evening planning out what I would say to her when I walked in today.

Hi Charlie, do you like peanut butter? Because I made twelve peanut butter and jelly sandwiches during a stressful moment in the middle of the night and thought you could have half of them.

Nothing about that seemed interesting enough to share, however.

Hi Charlie, I saw a dead snake in the woods behind my house and thought, wow, Charlie would hate this.

An obvious no.

Hi Charlie, who is the better singer, Freddie Mercury or Paul McCartney?

That was the best option I came up with, but it still seemed too random a topic to greet her with.

I even considered taking her flowers, but since our messages never moved past playful banter, I decided against it. The last thing I want to do is scare her away.

It seems my fears were unwarranted, however, because when I enter the library on Monday around noon, Mylo is behind the desk and Charlie is nowhere in sight.

"Are you sure it's mold?" Mylo says into his cell phone. He looks down at his watch and audibly groans as he gives me a frustrated look. "Fine. I can get there in ten minutes."

He disconnects the call and throws up his hands. "Zev, I'm glad you're here. I need your help."

"Okay," I reply hesitantly. "I don't know how to run a library, so please don't ask me to do that."

"No, nothing like that," Mylo says with a chuckle. "I need to go over to our new house. The contractor says he found mold in the garage. Sam is working at the newspaper and can't step away."

I wait for the favor. He still hasn't revealed it, which has me worried it's something big that I can't handle.

Vekkanaru xin. Useless.

That's what our handlers used to call me. When I had trouble in battle and one of my brothers needed to assist me with a kill, I knew the moment we returned to the laboratory we called home that the word would be shouted in my ear in between beatings. I would attempt to explain why I felt the life I was ordered to take should be spared, and my handlers would take turns lashing my back with heavy chains.

Useless. The word planted itself so deeply inside my brain matter that I still hear it whenever I'm faced with a new task.

"Charlie is at a doctor's appointment, but I told her I'd keep an eye on Nia while she's gone. She should be back soon, I think, but I need to leave now. Can you do it?"

A child? Me spending time alone with a child? "No, I don't think I can."

His face falls. "Come on. Why not?"

Children make me nervous. They tend to be more honest than adult humans, which I can appreciate, but since most adult humans find me odd, what would a child say? I came across one in an elevator once, a girl, sitting in her stroller with her mother focused primarily on her phone. It was just the three of us, and when I stepped inside, the child looked at me with a cold glare and pointed her small finger in my direction. She said nothing, just continued to stare and point until I left. It was unsettling.

What am I supposed to do with a child? There's so much they don't yet know. What would we talk about? Plus, they're so fragile. What am I supposed to do if Charlie's daughter falls and breaks several bones while under my care? How would I explain that? She would never forgive me.

Useless. Useless, useless, useless.

Swallowing the lump in my throat, I say, "I don't think I'll be good at this."

"That's what you're worried about?" Mylo asks with a wide grin. A grin so wide, it's clear I haven't convinced him I'm the wrong person for this job. "Zev, you're an artist. You have a creative mind. Just take Nia into the conference room and color. You'll be fine."

No. No, no, no. This is bad. "Doesn't Charlie have family who can watch her child?"

Mylo throws an arm around my shoulder and drags me over to the Storytime Corner section of the library where a small girl sits and flips through the pages of a picture book. "Charlie's dad is busy, that's why she brought Nia in with her today. You'll be doing her a huge favor by watching Nia, and it's a chance to get to know the most important person in your mate's life."

I pull back to look at him, shocked by his words.

"Oh, did you think you were hiding your obvious love for her?"

"No," I begin, unsure of what to say. "I wasn't hiding it, exactly…" I trail off. I've known Charlie is my mate for some time now, but I haven't shared that with anyone. It's jarring to hear it from someone else's lips.

"Well, now's your chance to solidify that bond." He gives my back a swift pat that I know is meant to be encouraging. "In order to win Charlie's heart, you need that child to love you. Get to work. I will be back as soon as I can."

"Wait," I plea, "shouldn't you introduce us?"

"Ah, yes, yes. My mistake," Mylo says. "Hey, Nia?"

The girl looks up and offers Mylo a bright, toothy smile.

"This is my brother, Zev. Zev, this is Nia."

I lift my hand and wave slowly, so as not to frighten her. "Hello. Pleased to meet you."

Mylo nods emphatically. His movements are big and animated in front of the child. If I were her, I'd find them off-putting, but Nia doesn't seem to mind. "Zev is going to stay with you for a bit while I check on something at home. Is that okay?"

"Thas okay," she says, her voice soft and delicate like a freshly bloomed flower.

My brother claps his hands together happily. "Why don't you two go into the big room and color for a while, huh? There's already some crayons and coloring books on the table."

Nia sticks a finger in her mouth and tilts her head to the side. "Is Mommy coming back soon?"

Splendid. She's dreading this as much as I am.

"She is indeed," Mylo vows. "But until then, you can show Zev how to color inside the lines."

I scoff. "I do not color outside the lines."

Mylo pinches my shoulder hard enough to make me wince as he keeps his gaze on Nia. "Can you do that for me?"

Nia nods and pulls her finger out of her mouth seconds before using the same hand to reach for mine. I feel her saliva coat my palm as she tugs me toward the conference room. My chest suddenly feels tight as I ponder how many germs now cover my skin. "But what about the desk?" I call out over my shoulder. It's my last opportunity to get out of this. "Doesn't someone need to watch the desk?"

"Our volunteer, Whitney, will man the desk. Don't worry about that," Mylo says, laughing heartily, likely at the panic he must see on my face. "Have fun, brother."

The door to the conference room closes behind me before I can offer another reason why I shouldn't be doing this, and suddenly I'm alone with Nia, and I have no idea what I'm supposed to do.

Luckily, Nia doesn't seem to be waiting for my cue. She heads straight for the stack of blank paper in the corner of the room, grabs a handful, and climbs into the rolling chair at the head of the table. She starts scribbling away with the crayons before she recalls my presence. "Come," she says, patting the seat next to her. "Sit here."

I do as she says, somewhat relieved to follow her commands. If she's the one deciding what we do, that makes my life much easier.

The next several minutes pass quickly as we draw on our respective pages; the only sounds in the room are her off-key but endearing humming and crayons rubbing on paper.

Eventually, she looks up from her paper and gasps at the sight of mine. "Wow! Is that a tiger?" she asks, pulling herself onto her knees in the chair to get a better look.

"Yes," I tell her. I've drawn a male tiger sitting tall on top of a boulder, his long pink tongue pressed against the edge of his paw as he cleans it. "I like their stripes."

Nia chuckles. "Me too. Their stripes are pretty."

"Their stripes help them hide in the wild," I explain. "They act as camouflage so the tiger can avoid predators and ambush their prey."

"Really?" she replies.

"They are big cats with soft toe pads that help them move through their environment quietly."

After a moment of her staring at my drawing, she asks, "Are tigers mean?"

"No, I don't think so," I tell her. "A vindictive spirit isn't something they possess. Like all other animals, they're just trying to survive. Everything they do is about survival. They're strong, and if they feel threatened, they will attack, but only because they need to protect themselves or their family."

"What does *vindick-vindickavive* mean?" she asks, stumbling over the word.

"Cruel or evil. Do you know what those words mean?"

She nods. "Like the Evil Queen in *Snow White.*"

I'm not familiar with that character, but if *evil* is part of her name, I'm sure she's right. "Yes, Nia. That's correct."

As she resumes her humming, I look at her drawing, and the crayon falls from my grasp. "What are you drawing? Is that…"

"Thas Otto," she says, filling in the creature's scales with a bright pink color. "My dragon."

"Your…dragon, you said?" Is this real? Am I dreaming? Is my mate's daughter drawing a dragon right before my eyes?

"Mmm-hmm."

"You like dragons?"

"Mm," is all she says.

That's not enough. I need to know everything. The how, the why, and where she was introduced to the creature I become in the shadows. But I must be careful with my line of questioning. Or should I? How perceptive are children at her age? I don't know what age she is, but would she notice my obvious interest in the subject and then proceed to judge me for it?

You need this child to love you.

Mylo's words from earlier pop back into my mind, and I decide to play it cool. Well, as cool as I am capable of being.

I clear my throat and wipe the sweat from my palms. "What do you like about them?"

She doesn't look up from her drawing as she adds a long stream of fire shooting out of its mouth, hitting the corner of the page. "I like how they can fly and how they, um, breathe fire and protect their friends and how pretty their wings are and, um, they have horns."

"They protect their friends?"

Nia nods. "Like Toothless and Elliot and Falkor and Sisu and Otto."

I don't understand. "These are dragons from stories?"

"Mmm-hmm. Well, not Otto. Otto is my friend. He's at home on the couch. But he keeps the bad dreams away. He's my soft dragon friend."

This must be a toy of some kind. There's no way Nia has a dragon she keeps in her home that is also small and docile enough to lie on a couch, right?

As far as my brothers and I know, we are the only draxilios in this area. I suppose there could be others in America, but we have not felt their presence. During his honeymoon in Italy, Mylo discovered others who felt like they could be similar to our kind, but he and Sam left the area before they could meet them.

If there was another dragon living in the town of Sudbury, big or small, surely, I would know about it. Charlie and Nia would be covered in their scent, and I have yet to notice any scent beyond the warm cinnamon and apple fragrance emanating from Charlie's smooth skin.

"I'm glad you have Otto," I tell Nia with a relieved sigh. "You do not deserve to have bad dreams."

"I know."

The yellow crayon snaps beneath her tight grip, and her eyes widen in panic at the sight. "Oh no. I'm sorry. I dint mean to."

These are not my crayons, but this hardly seems like a crisis. "Do not worry. It's just a crayon." I take the black one I was using to fill in the tiger's stripes and break it in half. "See?"

She giggles wildly as she reaches for the orange crayon and breaks it. Her joy is contagious. Breaking a crayon should not make me laugh, but when she starts laughing, I can't seem to help myself. We take turns breaking six more crayons, then, as I notice the number of whole crayons starting to dwindle, I say, "Okay, let's leave some of these in one piece."

When her laughter ceases, she inspects my hair closely. "Your bun is loose."

I drop my crayon and reach up to check my hair, and sure enough, several front pieces hang around my ears. "Thank you," I tell her before pulling the elastic free and throwing my hair into a cleaner, tighter knot atop my head.

I find I quite enjoy being in Nia's presence. She asks questions freely and doesn't shy away from sharing her opinions. At one point, she asks why I scribbled all over my hands, and I explain they are tattoos I did myself.

"Do you like them?" I ask.

"No," she replies plainly.

She doesn't engage in verbal trickery like adult humans often do. Where most would feel compelled to lie and say they like my tattoos, Nia offered her thoughts without hesitation. I appreciate that. She doesn't need to like my tattoos as they are mine alone, and I don't take it personally that her tastes differ from mine.

Perhaps all children are this way, but in the short time I've been with her, I've grown both fond and protective of Nia. Hearing that she has bad dreams bothers me because such a sweet, innocent being should never experience such a thing. Her rest should be nothing but peaceful, her mind filled with only calming imagery.

"Mommy!" Nia shouts as she leaps from the chair and runs toward the door.

I leap a bit myself, not realizing Charlie was here. "Oh, I, um… Mylo had to leave, and he said it would be okay if I watched Nia, and I wondered if—"

"Thank you so much," Charlie cuts in as she hauls Nia into her arms. "Whitney told me Mylo's dealing with a mold issue at the new house. I'm glad you came in today. Not sure what I would've done otherwise." She pulls back and looks at Nia. "Aren't we glad Zev was here?"

Nia wiggles out of Charlie's arms and slides down the front of her body until her feet touch the ground. "Mommy, look at what Zev made." She grabs my tiger drawing and holds it up proudly.

"Wow, that's incredible," Charlie says, her tone genuine as she admires my sketch. "And what did you draw, Little Mama?"

She skips around my chair over to hers and grabs her drawing in her small fist. Charlie takes it and carefully uncrumples it.

"Aww, it's Otto," she says with a smile. "Very good, baby." Her gaze finds mine, and I lose myself in it. "I'm sorry you had to interrupt your day to babysit, but really, I so appreciate..." her gaze shifts to my left. "Why are there so many broken crayons in here?"

"It's no problem," I answer quickly, hoping to distract her from the Crayola massacre on the table. "I had fun." The moment the words are out, I'm surprised by the truth in them. What seemed like such a daunting task not even an hour ago has become something I'm eager to do again.

"Say thank you to Mr. Zev for drawing with you today, okay?"

It's over? So soon? But I don't want to say goodbye to Nia. I could stay in here and color with her for the rest of the day. In fact, I'd prefer it.

"Thank you, Zev," Nia says as she wraps her little arms around my neck and squeezes. "Shine bright."

"Shine...bright?" I repeat, confused.

Charlie chuckles. "That's just something I say to her every day before school."

Something shifts inside my chest during Nia's embrace. At first, it feels as if a crack has formed, and I expect pain to follow. When it doesn't, I notice a different sensation. It's akin to expansion, though I have no idea how that could be possible. Confused, I press my hand over my heart and rub small circles into it as Nia and Charlie say goodbye and leave the room.

It isn't until my eyes begin to itch that I understand what's happening, and how irrevocably my life has changed. Soon—it may take seconds, or minutes—my eyes will turn blood red, indicating that my heart is no longer mine. It now belongs to not one human, but two.

CHAPTER 6

CHARLIE

I haven't seen Zev in over a week, and I don't understand it. He sent me a message saying he was sick last week and couldn't make it to class, even though I saw him that very day when he watched Nia at the library. But fine, whatever. When you're sick, you're sick. I sent him a few mood-boosting songs over the days that followed, none of which he responded to. Then he skipped last night's class, and I've been anxiously obsessing about his absence ever since.

"Charlie!" Vanessa shouts when I walk into Tipsy's. This girls' night could not have come at a better time.

Sam waves me over excitedly. "That dress is giving disco fever. Give us a spin."

Preening, I twirl around and then give them each a hug. "Hey, guys. Thanks for pushing me to come out."

Izzy greets me by asking what I'll have. All business, this one.

"Whiskey sour with three cherries, please."

They nod and get right to mixing my drink.

"How are things?" Vanessa asks when I take the empty seat between her and Sam.

I let out a heavy sigh. "Not the best, to be honest. I'm just stressed at the moment." Stressed about lots of things—my financial status,

HER ALIEN STUDENT | 47

which is broke, a safe and affordable apartment I can't seem to find in this town, and most of all, Zev.

I thought maybe he was resting, so I left him alone. The last thing I want when I'm sick is my phone blowing up with messages, so I didn't bother him after that. But when he skipped last night's class and responded to my email this morning asking if he was okay with nothing but a "Sorry. Not sure when I'll return," my mind really started spinning.

Does he hate me? Is he dead and his murderer is replying to his emails to cover his tracks? Was watching Nia so terrible that he decided to avoid me forever?

It's not like I scolded him about the crayons he and Nia destroyed—though I should've because art supplies aren't cheap. When Nia told me they sat there breaking crayons for no good reason, I about lost my damn mind. It's not like Zev knew I was mad about it though.

I don't get it. I thought we had something, or that we were in the process of having something. Or, at the very least, I thought we were friends.

Did I make it up or misread the situation?

Maybe he's ghosting me. I haven't dated many guys since Nia was born, but there were two that disappeared off the face of the earth after I told them I'm a mom. Zev didn't seem like the kind of guy who would pull this shit, but I shouldn't be shocked by this nonsense anymore. That's just men, and obviously, Zev is like the rest of them.

"Spill," Sam says, taking a big swig of her cocktail. "We can help."

Vanessa nods emphatically.

Instead of sharing the details of the whole Zev conundrum, I pull out my phone and show them the apartment listings I've been eyeing. "I went to see this one yesterday. It was…fine, but I'm pretty sure there was a drug deal happening by the dumpster as I was leaving."

Sam scrolls to the map section of the listing. "Oh yeah, that's a bad part of town. Let's go ahead and veto that one right now."

Pulling up the next link, I go through the pics slowly. It's a two-unit building that was recently renovated. "This one has a walk-in closet, and I'd get my own bathroom, which is way more than I currently have at my dad's place."

Vanessa gasps at the address. "Shit, isn't that the house where Mrs. Levine was murdered?"

"Eek, yeah it is," Sam adds. "But that was twenty years ago, and it's been renovated, so you're probably fine."

I'm confused by her logic. "What does tha—"

"It doesn't matter if it's been renovated," Vanessa interrupts. "Ghosts stay with the original structure."

Sam shakes her head. "No, they don't. Gutting the inside of a house gets rid of any ghosts."

Vanessa's eyes roll. "If the bones remain, the ghosts remain."

No walk-in closet or en suite bathroom is worth having an evil spirit as a roommate. "Forget it."

Next, I show them two apartments in the same building that seem overpriced, considering the outdated fixtures and tiny bedrooms. I could probably make either one work if I had to, but my finances would be stretched super thin, even more so than they already are. They agree that they're not worth the price, and also point out that both units face the abandoned train tracks that cut through town, which gives me the willies.

"I wish I knew you were looking for a place," Sam says, using her straw to push around the ice in her drink to create an extra sip. "We just sold my mom's condo for next to nothing."

"Oh yeah? Are you and Mylo staying there until it closes?" Izzy asks, sliding my whiskey sour across the bar. "Or are you staying at his place?"

Sam orders a refill. "We have to be out in two weeks, but the renovations in the new place are coming along. The contractors found mold in the garage, but luckily, they were able to remove it without tearing the whole thing down. In fact, we're going to throw a Halloween party to celebrate. That'll be our housewarming."

"Ooh yay. Can I dress up as a tired preggo?" Vanessa asks.

Sam looks her up and down. "So you'll just wear that?"

"Yep," Vanessa nods with a proud smirk. "Exactly."

"Of course. You look scrumptious."

"I'm surprised you're having trouble finding a place," Vanessa says, shifting the subject back. "It's not like this is an expensive area."

Izzy clears their throat. "Housing options are crap around here because of all the people who came in snapped up the affordable options and turned them into vacation rentals. They charge a fortune to the leaf-peepers, and the rest of us are left with nothing."

I hadn't considered that, but it makes sense. "Well, I'm screwed."

"If you're in a jam, there's a studio upstairs you can crash in," Izzy offers. "I sometimes sleep there if I have to close one day and open the next, but it's yours if you want it. The floor isn't soundproof though, so it can get kind of noisy with us right below."

"Thanks, Izzy. I appreciate the offer," I tell them. "Nia has enough trouble sleeping through the night as it is, so I don't think that'll work."

"No worries. If you change your mind, just let me know and it's yours."

Commotion by the entrance draws our attention, and it's Caitlyn, tripping over her own feet. She stumbles over to us, and Sam asks Izzy if they can bring her refill and make it a double.

"Ladiesss," Caitlyn slurs, tossing her arms over mine and Vanessa's shoulders. Vanessa immediately pushes her off, and she leans heavily against me, her breath thick with wine and her teeth stained red. "Look at ush, just like the good ol' days. Next round isson me."

"How are you possibly this drunk already?" Sam asks, her tone like ice. "Did you pregame at home like a college freshman?"

"Actually, no, Samantha. I've been on a solo bar crawl, and I must say..." she trails off, staring distantly at something behind us. Sam, Vanessa, and I look at each other, wondering if she's ever going to finish her sentence. Finally, her gaze meets mine, and she snaps out of it with a burp. "It's been an absolute blast."

Vanessa's brow lifts as she contemplates this. "A bar crawl? There are only a few bars in this town, and none of them are within walking distance of each other."

"My nephew is an Uber driver. He usually stays near Manchester for his shifts, but he knows Tuesday is my bar night, so he doesn't stray too far."

Caitlyn waves Izzy over and orders four lemon drops. When Izzy lines them up in front of us, Vanessa pushes hers away. "Caitlyn, I'm pregnant. Plus, the smell of that is making me gag."

Without waiting even a second, Caitlyn downs hers, then smiles gleefully as she takes Vanessa's. "More for me then."

Sam hesitates, but then grumbles, "Whatever. The least you can do is pay for my drink."

I really don't want mine. I'm not a shot person, but it's clear Caitlyn is trying to make amends, and since I'm not caught up in the drama between her and the other girls, I refuse to make this moment more awkward than it already is. My throat burns as the bitter liquid slides down my throat, and I wave both hands in front of my glass when Izzy comes over. "No more for me. I make terrible decisions when I'm drunk, so I'm done for the night."

"What exactly do you want from us, Caitlyn?" Sam asks. "You trying to get back in with Beth by digging up dirt on us?"

Caitlyn vehemently shakes her head no. "Beth and I are done. Not on speaking terms."

"Then what?" Vanessa asks.

"Is it so unthinkable that I just want to be friends with you?"

Sam and Vanessa exchange a wary glance. "Why would we do that?" Sam asks, but it comes out more statement than question. Her posture is stiff and guarded as she addresses Caitlyn with a curled lip of contempt. "You took Beth's side during the most painful moment of Vanessa's life. And when she mocked my mom's Alzheimer's, you stood there and said nothing. So why would we even consider getting close to you again? What do you bring to the table?"

"Well, as town clerk, I've gotten pretty tight with members of the council and all the local judges. We're like this," she says, crossing her fingers. "In fact, with some of them, it's more like this…" Caitlyn proceeds to make a sexual gesture with one finger and thumb forming a circle while poking her other pointer finger through it.

"Ugh, seriously?" Vanessa says, looking positively disgusted. "Aren't most of the guys on city council really old? And married?"

Caitlyn waves a dismissive hand. "I was married for thirteen years, and we didn't have sex for the last five. I finally get to sow my oats. Don't fucking judge me."

Sam rubs small circles into her temple. "My god, nobody cares about the Viagra-powered dicks you're sucking. Just get on with it."

"If you'd let me finish," Caitlyn shouts, her spit spraying across the bar top. Izzy comes over wearing a frosty expression and wipes it up. The look goes over Caitlyn's head, and upon Izzy's approach, she orders a glass of "the cheapest bottle of Merlot you have."

"You're losing us," Vanessa warns Caitlyn.

"Grady Vincent just happens to be the owner of one of those dicks," Caitlyn says conspiratorially, "and I've heard he's been giving you guys hell with the book review."

That certainly piques my interest. "So, you're saying if we agree to hang out with you, you'll get Vincent to back off?"

"It's not like he actually cares about this shit," she says to Sam. "He's just doing it because he's friends with Burton and Burton hates your husbands. And I'm not even asking for that much," she clarifies. "If I get him to stop the book review, we're square. All the times I stood by when Beth was acting like a total cunt—we put that behind us. Let it go. Consider it my official olive branch."

"Why would he do that for you?" Sam asks. "He doesn't seem like the type to hand out favors. What's your leverage?"

Caitlyn's expression turns coy. "Let's just say there's *something* I do for him that his wife refuses to do, and let's just say that *something* would really embarrass him if it were made public."

Sam lets out an exaggerated fake yawn. "Pegging? It's pegging, isn't it? That's not as shocking as you think it is. Men and women everywhere enjoy a little ass play."

"Is that so?" Vanessa asks with a smirk. "Are you saying you and Mylo are among these men and women?"

Sam pauses as she stares at Vanessa, blood rushing to her cheeks.

"If you want details, I'll give you details, but only when this one leaves," she says, pointing to Caitlyn.

I absolutely do not want details of what my boss prefers in bed.

"Okay, fine. You might not find it shocking," Caitlyn says, "but he thinks his constituents would, and it's something he's very private about. There's also some... role play we do that I'm pretty sure would fuck up his whole universe if anyone found out about it, so the point is, yes, I have leverage. Buckets of it."

I send Sam a pleading look. Whatever happened between Sam, Vanessa, and Caitlyn, as bad as it was, is in the past. This book review Councilman Vincent has put us through has been a nightmare, and I know if Mylo were here, he'd be begging Sam to agree to this just to make it stop.

Sam watches Caitlyn down her glass of wine in two swigs and looks as if she's about to decline her offer. I can't let that happen.

"Sam, come on," I beg. "This would be huge for us. Do it for Mylo. Think about how stressed he's been lately."

Vanessa leans in and lowers her voice, "We're not committing to a girls' trip or matching tattoos," she says, not so low that Caitlyn can't hear, but in a tone that indicates she's trying to infuse some logic. "Just moving forward. Letting go of the past."

Sam finishes her second drink and lets out a deep breath. "Fuck it. Fine."

Caitlyn squeals as she hops in place, thrilled about her victory. She starts to lose her footing, but I grab her arm before she falls flat on her ass. "Okay, I think maybe it's time to call it a night, yeah?" I say, waving Izzy over.

"Yep," Izzy says. "Sorry, Caitlyn. Afraid I have to cut you off. You want this on a card or are you paying with cash?"

Caitlyn pulls out her credit card and drops it on the bar. "I've got theirs too. This has been fun, ladies."

"Thank you," I tell Caitlyn, gesturing to her phone. "You want to text your nephew to come get you?"

She does, and once she settles her tab, the three of us walk Caitlyn outside to wait for her Uber. Her makeup is smudged, the lacy cup of her bra is peeking out of her top, and she can't even stand on her own. I'm glad we were here tonight, not only because it seems she's going to help get Vincent off our backs, but also because it's clear she needs someone watching hers.

Her nephew arrives a few minutes later, and Sam and I help Caitlyn climb into the back seat. As the car pulls away, my mind drifts to Zev, and the words just fall out. "Have you guys seen Zev lately? Is he okay?"

"Um, yeah, I saw him a few days ago," Sam says, suddenly avoiding my gaze and nervously scratching her cheek. "Seemed fine."

Vanessa's eyes meet mine, but her expression is tight, and it looks like she's screaming internally. "I think he was under the weather for a bit there, right, Sam?"

"Oh yeah. He had a cold or something."

They know something. That much is obvious. But what's also obvious is that they're not gonna crack, either because they want to protect their brother-in-law, or because they know he's blowing me off and they don't want to be responsible for my shattered ego. Either way, I get it. I nod and drop the subject.

We go back into Tipsy's for a final drink, mine being Sprite, and then go our separate ways. When I get home, Dad and Joyce are watching a movie in the living room. I say goodnight to them, kiss my sleeping Nia on the cheek, and get ready for bed. I check my DMs, hoping for a new one from Zev, and my heart sinks into my stomach when there isn't.

When I wake the next morning, I don't feel better necessarily, but I am determined to stop worrying about Zev and focus on finding a new place for me and Nia. A fresh start.

Dad and Joyce head out for their walk to the coffee shop, and I drop Nia off at school. When I get home, there's a car I don't recognize in the driveway. It's a black Mercedes sedan with Massachusetts plates. I get out of my car and do a slow lap around it, gaining no new information until I hear a voice near the front door.

"There you are," the voice says. I know that voice. I hate that voice.

When he pops his head around the side of the house, I feel my blood begin to boil. He shouldn't be here. More importantly, how did he find me?

"Evan?"

He comes into view, and I wish I was holding a baseball bat or something I could use as a weapon. "What the fuck are you doing here?"

He shoves a colorful bouquet of flowers at me, and when I don't take them, he shrugs and places them on the doormat. "I'm here to see my daughter."

CHAPTER 7

CHARLIE

"She's not your daughter," I say, pushing past him toward the door. He doesn't deserve my attention or a moment of my time.

"Let's not do this dance," he replies, smoothing back his gelled blond hair with his hand and adjusting the paisley blue tie that matches his navy-blue suit. "Look, I know she's mine. We were together, then, out of nowhere, you quit the campaign, dumped me, and ran off. Nine months later, you give birth a thousand miles away to a bouncing baby girl with my nose, my cheekbones, and my smile."

When I don't say anything, he shrugs. "I'm happy to take a paternity test, if that's what it takes."

"Fine," I shout, knowing he's got me. "You played a very small role in Nia's creation. Thanks for your sperm. Time to go."

He crosses his arms and laughs. "No, no, no. I'm here for the long haul."

"Why?" I ask. "Why now? What could you possibly want from us after all this time? And how did you even find us?"

"I'm a congressman, Charlotte. It's not difficult to get what I want." He smiles, and the sight of it makes my stomach turn.

How did I ever find that smile attractive? He looks like his dad is

The Joker. Actually, I know how. It's because he's an exceptional liar and a narcissist. I was the newly appointed chief of staff to the mayor, and he was the press secretary. We worked together closely, performing high-stress jobs that required long hours and late nights. He lured me in with praise and false promises, then slowly chipped away at my confidence, my sense of reality, and isolated me from everyone I felt close to.

"My condolences to the people in your district," I say in a biting tone.

He throws his head back and howls with laughter. "I've always loved your feisty side. Why don't we go inside and hash this out?" When he takes a step toward the door, I block his path.

"No, we're going to stay right here. Just tell me what you want."

"I told you. I want to see my daughter."

"Why?"

He sighs. "Well, truth be told, I'm up for re-election next year, and my campaign manager is concerned about my lack of appeal to Black voters."

"I can see that," I tell him with a proud nod. "You've got a real Klan vibe about you."

"Very funny," he says with a smirk. "Finley and I are married now with a baby on the way, but if the people in my district were to see me on the campaign trail with my Black daughter, I think it would really improve my numbers. You know? A real modern American family."

I wasn't expecting him to be so forthcoming with his shady plans, but I guess I shouldn't be surprised. This is the same man who threw books at me when he thought I was flirting with a colleague and when I showed him the bruises on my arms, he said I shouldn't have made him jealous.

"You want to use our daughter as a prop? Okay, take your gas station flowers and your skinny suit pants and get the fuck off my property."

"Hmm, you mean your dad's property, right?" He takes a menacing step closer. "Because you don't own this house. No, this house is owned by Darius Brooks. That's your dad, right? You haven't purchased or even rented a property since Nia was born." Another step. "You've lived with your cousins in Houston—that's where you gave birth, wasn't it?—your old college roommate in Park City, another friend in Danbury, Connecticut, you couch-surfed with a few people in Boston when Nia was around three, back to Park City for a bit, and now, here." Evan lifts his nose to the sky and takes a deep inhale. "And this place is the biggest shithole of them all."

I had a feeling he was keeping tabs on me, though I tried to never stick around any of those places long enough for him to find me. But Evan craves control above all else, so the fact that he knows every place I've lived, and with whom, isn't a shock to me. It's terrifying, of course, but a shock? No.

This is just who he is, and why, when I found out I was pregnant with his child, I packed my shit and ran as fast as my feet would take me. I wanted the baby I carried, loved her from the moment I heard her little heart beating so strongly inside my belly. But the only way I would've been able to do this was if I kept him far, far away from us. That meant constantly looking over my shoulder; it meant never staying in one place for too long.

In Houston, when Nia was about six months old, a box of shredded red roses showed up at my cousin's house. The note said, "Run all you want. You will never not be mine." Evan didn't need to sign it for me to know he was the sender. He bought me a bouquet of roses after each fight we had that resulted in bruises covering my skin. That was his signature move. His way of apologizing and promising it would never happen again. During our relationship, I received seven of those *I'll never hurt you again* bouquets. The flowers are long gone, and the bruises have since faded, but the pain and fear are still fresh.

I used to love long-stemmed red roses. Now the sight of them makes me sick.

Sure, things haven't exactly been stable, but Nia and I have fared just fine. I'm all she needs.

I take a step back, putting some distance between us. "I happen to like it here. Nia does too. She's thriving, actually, and I'm not sure taking her out of school so you can Lion King her all over western

New Jersey is what's best for her right now. So thanks for stopping by, but it's time to go."

He shoves his hands in his pockets and rocks back and forth on his heels. "I was really hoping we wouldn't have to involve the courts, but if that's what you want to do…"

"You're seriously threatening me right now? What, you want custody? You think a judge will let you within ten feet of my daughter after what you just admitted?"

"Please. It's my word against yours," he scoffs. "Who do you think the judge will believe? The hardworking public servant? The married man with a mortgage? Or the vengeful ex-girlfriend who can't hold down a job or a place to live for more than a year at a time?"

I can't help but gasp at his audacity, and the fear that he might be even the tiniest bit right.

"I'm just a man who didn't know he was a father," Evan continues, his fist pressed against his chest as he practices looking forlorn. He must've spent hours in the mirror trying to get it right. Genuine emotion is not something that comes naturally to him. "And now that I know, I want my beautiful daughter to have the best life possible. That's what I can give her." He pauses, holding my gaze, then lets out a sinister chuckle. "I'm still working out the kinks, but it'll go something like that."

"You are unbelievable."

"I bet your dad would even take my side on this," he says, looking around me to peek through the living room window. "Is he home, by the way?"

"No, he isn't," I tell him, stepping to the side to block his view. Dad really isn't home, but I don't need this creepy bastard looking inside my house. "And he would never take your side. Not over his own daughter's. Are you out of your fucking mind?"

Even as I say it, I'm not so sure. I'd like to think Dad would be on my side and threaten to smash Evan's face against the sidewalk for looking at me wrong, but I don't know. This is a seriously manipulative man. What if he does push for custody? I can't afford to go to court over this. I can barely afford that stupid ticket for my expired car registration.

"I'm going to be in town for as long as it takes, Charlotte," he warns. "You've always been difficult, but I'm ready for a fight."

If that does happen…if he sues me for custody, I need people on my side. My dad could be a character witness for me, and he could explain to the judge that Evan is dangerous and shouldn't be anywhere near us. I just need my dad to see Evan for who and what he truly is.

"Fine, come to dinner tonight. Six-thirty," I shout, my voice high and panicked. "Don't be late."

"Lovely," Evan mutters, putting on his sunglasses and striding confidently toward his car. "See you then."

The moment his Mercedes is out of view, my purse lands at my feet with a thud, and my knees buckle. I can't catch my breath, and little black dots appear before my eyes. What have I done? But really, what could I have done? He didn't give me a choice.

That man, that *monster*, came here threatening to take my baby girl from me. I can't let him win.

He's right though. Not about everything, but about how I would look to a judge. A flaky, unstable woman who'd rather run all over the country than let the biological father of her child spend time with her? If Evan spins his web of lies, I'm sure that's what the judge will think.

This dinner has to go well. I need Dad on my side. He's all I've got.

* * *

Evan shows up twenty minutes early with a bottle of wine, a forty of Olde English for my dad, and a bag of Skittles for Nia, because he's two parts asshole, one part racist, and one part clueless. I didn't discover the racist part of him until after we started dating, and by then, I was so deep inside the cycle of abuse that I couldn't get out. The fact that he has another child on the way makes me deeply concerned for that child and everyone forced to interact with him or her.

My dad thanks Evan for the beer and immediately proceeds to pour it down the drain in front of him, which gives me hope.

Evan and I agreed the moment he stepped over the threshold that we would refer to him as Mommy's friend in front of Nia because there's no good way to spring this monumental news on her without it being traumatic. "For today. Just today," Evan conceded.

I also agreed to have his name added to Nia's birth certificate, rather than wait for him to sue me for paternity. If this does turn into a custody fight, I don't want the judge to see me as some difficult, vengeful ex. This is about Nia's protection, and she's safe with me, not him. I'm sure I can show the judge that.

"Well, I'm looking forward to this. I haven't had a home-cooked meal in weeks," Evan complains. "My wife is pregnant and hasn't been in the mood to cook."

"Hmm," I say, turning to my left so I can really look at him. "Seems like you have two working hands. You couldn't whip something up for yourself? Or maybe for the woman growing your child?"

My dad chuckles as he stabs a meatball and several pieces of penne with his fork and takes a bite.

Nia pushes her noodles around through the sauce, quietly humming. She doesn't understand what's going on here, and for that, I'm grateful. Let her think this boring white guy in the ill-fitting suit is just Mommy's friend. Then, hopefully, she'll never have to see him again. Fine with me.

"Thank you so much for having me, Mr. Brooks. I've been eager to meet you, and of course, Nia, for quite some time," Evan says, ignoring my comment and turning on the charm. "I know my absence has been felt, and if there's anything I could do to go back and change that, I would."

"Yeah, well, it seems awfully convenient timing for you to show up now," Dad says, "with your term ending and Black voters not turning out for you."

Yes, Dad. Get him.

Obviously, I prepped him for this conversation. I told him about the emotional abuse. Not about the physical abuse, because I wasn't sure how he would handle it, and also because I didn't want to relive it in front of him. But even without the horrifying details, Dad promised he'd have my back tonight.

Evan's face scrunches with confusion. "Hmm, I'm not sure where you heard that, but I've polled exceptionally well among Black voters. In fact, I've made significant progress in addressing income inequality and housing insecurity in my district. I was also instrumental in getting a new mental health facility opened this year. Black voters were key to my victory in the last election, and I'm confident I'll have their support this next time around."

My mouth falls open. "That's not...that's not what you said." He looks at me like I'm wearing clown makeup and a giant, honkable red nose. "You told me earlier tha—"

"I'm sorry if you misheard me, Charlotte," he says, his voice thick with concern as he puts a hand on my shoulder. I brush him off and he turns back to face my father. "Mr. Brooks, I understand your hesitation to trust me. I would feel the exact same way. Some guy just shows up out of the blue five years later and wants a relationship with his kid? It sounds shady."

My dad grunts in agreement. "It sure does."

"I'm not a perfect man, and I don't proclaim to be."

Understatement of the fucking millennium.

"I've made many mistakes," he continues, "but I had a health scare recently that put things in perspective, and I don't know..." he trails off, looking almost choked up.

He should get an Oscar for this performance.

"It-it just woke me up to the harsh reality that life is short, you know? It's tragically short, and if I don't start prioritizing the important things, my children and my wife, then it's going to pass me by, and I'll be filled with regrets." He takes a sip of wine, closes his eyes, and shakes his head as if he's lost in that very realization, as if it's hitting him hard right in front of us, and it's not a complete load of crap. "I don't want to be filled with regrets, sir."

Dad drops his head and nods solemnly. "I get that."

Nia tilts her head as she looks at Evan. "Who are you again?"

God bless this child and her nose for bullshit. She definitely got that from me.

Evan gives her a tight smile. "I'm your—"

"My friend," I finish for him. I'm not letting him share anything I don't want him to. "He's my friend."

She takes a bite of pasta. "He doesn't seem like your friend."

Because he's not, I want to say. *He's technically your father but also my mortal enemy.*

"And what's your plan? To make up for the time you lost, I mean?" Dad asks, not looking nearly as repulsed by Evan as he should. My heart rate goes from zero to sixty. "My daughter works hard to protect and support Nia. How do you plan to contribute?"

Okay, better.

"I want to assure you that I have no intention of disrupting your granddaughter's life," he says, sounding surprisingly earnest for such a fucking snake. "The only thing I want to do is improve it. Her life and Charlotte's. I can't imagine how difficult it's been for Charlotte to do this on her own."

Dad sighs. "It has been." His gaze flicks between me and Evan. "You know, it's been hard to watch."

No. Is he falling for this? He can't be falling for this.

"The best part of this is that she doesn't have to anymore," Evan replies, using that politician's voice that's fueled with hope when there isn't any to be found. I half expect him to drop in America and freedom into the conversation to really sell it. "I want to be there. I want to be involved, and I want to help cover expenses. The only thing I want in return is quality time. That's it."

Dad looks at me, then his eyes drop to his plate. "It's something to think about."

What the fuck?

Evan shoots me that Joker smile and happily digs into his food. "Excellent. I'm so glad you agree."

Dinner passes at a snail's pace, and I have trouble finishing even half of what's on my plate. I can't get over how few insults my dad has delivered tonight, and how he's even smiled at Evan a few times.

Eventually, Evan hands me a piece of paper with his number on it, and says, "I'll be in town for the next two weeks, at least," loud enough so Dad can hear him in the kitchen. I slam the door behind him, lock it, and hurl myself on the loveseat.

"Thank god that's over," I say as I watch Nia pretend to fly Otto around the living room.

Dad comes in with another glass of wine and plops down in his recliner. "It wasn't so bad."

"Dad, what the hell? You said you were gonna back me up tonight. What about all the stuff I told you? Please don't tell me you bought that." Clearly, I should've told him about the physical abuse. The bruises. Then maybe he wouldn't be looking at me like Evan should become a frequent dinner guest. Over my rotting corpse.

"I know I've told you this story before, but it bears repeating," Dad says. "When I found out your mother was pregnant, I panicked. We got into an argument over whether she should get an abortion, and I left. I wasn't there for her during most of her pregnancy, and I look back at the time with so much regret, you know? I was a coward. An absolute coward. I hate myself for leaving her the way I did. She struggled when she didn't have to. If I could go back in time and give her the support she deserved, I would.

"And now I see my daughter, my only child, trying to do this alone, and she's drowning. You may not like him, but this man is throwing you a lifeline."

"Dad, that was such a long time ago, and you came back before I was born so you didn't let me down. You may have let Mom down, but you came back. It's forgotten," I tell him. It's not the first time I've heard this story, and I know it won't be the last. If he has regrets, fine, but I'm not going to let his decisions influence this one. Evan is nothing like my dad. He's Satan in a slim-fit suit. "I don't need Evan, and more importantly, I don't trust him."

"Well, you need someone. Someone other than me. I ain't gonna be here forever. That saying 'it takes a village,' that's the truth."

I've grown weary of that saying. "How am I supposed to afford a regular babysitter when I can't even afford my own apartment?"

"I'm not talking about a paid village. Only rich people can afford that. You're not Beyoncé."

No, I'm not. I'm certainly not.

"But you like it here, right?" Dad asks. "This is where you want to stay?"

I've been running for a long time, and it's gotten old. I'm tired of running. Plus, Evan found us, he seems to always know where we are, so running would be pointless. There's no reason to run anymore.

Sudbury is nice. I like working at the library and having Mylo as my boss. Sam and Vanessa are becoming close friends, and I might not have known them long, but I trust them.

Then there's Zev. Logically, he shouldn't be part of this equation. I know that. My brain fully recognizes that Zev has ghosted me and is no longer worth my time. But my heart, my stupid, stupid heart, still hopes he'll DM me with an elaborate and perfectly reasonable excuse for being MIA, and we can go back to being friends, or whatever we were.

"Yeah, I think so," I eventually say. "I want to stay."

"Then you need to start finding your people and make them your village. You don't want Evan to be part of that village? Fine. That's your call to make, but I know you're already making friends. Lean on them."

CHAPTER 8

ZEV

*C*harlie is my mate. She's my mate! I knew it the moment I met her, but I suppose it took meeting Nia for everything to click into place. The whites of my eyes have been blood red since the day Nia hugged me at the library. That was over a week ago, and I'm still not sure how to proceed.

Obviously, I couldn't attend class in this state, so I told Charlie I was sick. Since then, I've been scrambling to come up with a way to see her without the sight of me terrifying her. I've been too afraid to even message her back. I'm so desperate to be near her and Nia that I know I'll tell her I need to see her…and then what? No, I can't see her. Not until I come up with a way to hide my eyes.

"Okay," Luka, my eldest brother, says, coming into my bedroom with a package that just arrived. He opens it and examines the contents closely. "These are from Jay. He said they're colored contacts that he got from the dark web, which I suppose is an online shop of some kind."

"No," I protest, holding up my hands. "The last ones burned. It felt like my eyelids were melting off."

"These are different. Jay assured me they're better than the other ones."

I step in front of my floor-length mirror and carefully put the contacts in. They cover the entire eye, with the center being completely transparent, so they don't block my vision. "How are Jay and Talia doing?" I ask, waiting for the burning to start.

"Good, good," Luka says with a warm expression.

My brothers and I owe everything to Jay and Talia. The night we crashed on Earth, Jay was the first human we spoke to, and even though Luka used his power to influence Jay into giving us a place to sleep that night above his pawn shop in Boston, he also fed us each about a dozen tacos from Taco Bell, and he and Talia helped us get settled in this new world. We told them we had escaped from a cult, but they figured out we weren't human. It was never a discussion, but it was clear they knew we were different.

"They just adopted a ten-year-old girl, so now they have three kids, and their edible bakery has taken off. They're doing novelty cakes with THC for private parties and events."

"That's great," I tell Luka. "I miss them. They should come visit us."

Luka sighs. "I keep telling them that."

We continue looking at each other in the mirror until it starts to feel weird. "I'm hungry. Are you in the mood for Mexican? Talking about Jay put me in the mood for tacos."

"No, I'll pass. Harper texted saying she and Vanessa want pizza. I'm going to eat over there once they finish Vanessa's exam."

"Is Ryan here too?"

Luka looks appalled. "Of course. He's the one who'll deliver Vanessa's baby. We don't come up here anymore without him."

Harper is Luka's mate. She's a successful veterinarian and runs her practice in Salem, New Hampshire, where they live. Ryan is her head veterinary technician, and when Harper was pregnant with both of their boys, Ryan was the only one she could trust to deliver the babies. Going to a regular hospital was out of the question, given that the children are half-draxilio, and Ryan was the only one with enough medical expertise to do the job.

"And you guys don't mind staying at Vanessa and Axil's house?"

Luka has kept a bedroom here since we first bought the house, but since Vanessa and Axil got together and found out Vanessa is pregnant, Harper and Luka bring Ryan and their two sons, Hudson and Cooper, and stay over there. It's easier to keep the medical equipment in the same place, and there are plenty of bedrooms for everyone.

"Okay, I'm going to Pollo Palace. I'll let you know if my eyes start boiling."

Luka gives my shoulder an encouraging slap. "Keep your sunglasses on, just in case."

It's a nice day out, so I grab a seat at one of their outdoor tables and place a to-go order for three barbacoa burritos, a little gem salad, and a side of elote. After the server walks away, I contemplate ordering some chips and guacamole while I wait. Then I notice they offer three types of salsa on their menu, which sound equally delicious. Maybe I can add that to my or—

"Zev?"

Shit.

"Zev."

Charlie says my name again, and I foolishly pretend I don't hear her. For some reason, having my sunglasses on makes me feel like I might be invisible, which I am very much not. I wasn't prepared to see her today. I have the contacts in, but who knows how long they'll last? Or what kind of adverse reaction I might have while wearing them.

"Are you seriously ignoring me right now?" she asks, her voice breaking on the last word. She stomps over with her paper bag in hand and drops it in front of me. "Wow, I didn't want to think you were ghosting me. I thought, *oh, he's just sick. He's taking time to rest.* But look at you now. Looking perfectly fucking healthy and grabbing a bite to eat on this beautiful day."

"Charlie, it's not what you think."

"I'm such a jackass. We start sending each other songs and it felt like we were, I don't know, becoming friends," she says, her bottom lip trembling. "Like, real friends. Which is something I could really use right now."

I feel horrible. Tears leave wet trails down her cheeks, and I want nothing more than to wipe them away and tell her that the last nine days have been the worst of my life. That the distance between us has tormented me beyond anything my handlers ever did. I would take a lifetime of chain lashings over the hell that has been this time away from her and Nia.

They are my entire world now. I want nothing more than to be whatever they need. Make them laugh, make them smile, and give them enough comfort that Charlie never experiences a moment of stress for the rest of her days, and that Nia lives a long, fulfilling life without another bad dream.

I can't say any of this to Charlie, though, because she's human, and she won't understand. "I promise I wasn't ghosting you," I say instead. An excuse though? I don't have one to give her.

"Excuse me," I say, grabbing the attention of the closest server. "Can you please refund Ms. Brooks for her lunch and put the bill on my card instead? And, um," I look at Charlie, "do you enjoy margaritas? Because it says all over their menu that theirs are the best. May I buy you one? Please?"

She wipes her cheeks, clears her throat, and takes the seat across from me. "I like margaritas." Her mouth still forms a frown, but it's starting to flatten, and I feel utterly victorious.

I turn back to the server. "Then we shall have your largest pitcher, please, and thank you."

The server smiles and takes Charlie's bill and my credit card away with her.

I place my hands on the table. "I owe you an endless supply of apologies, so here is the first of many. I'm sorry. I am. There is no excuse for my behavior. But I cannot express how happy I am to see you today. Really, Charlie. I've missed talking to you and sharing songs." I don't know what I can say that will keep her here. Honesty is all I have, but is it enough? "Will you stay and eat lunch with me?"

She purses her lips as she considers my invitation. I don't expect her to agree. She has no reason to give me another chance after disappearing on her the way I did. My heart thumps against my chest, practically bursting through the bones as I wait patiently for her answer.

"Fine. Lunch and one drink," she says, tearing into her paper bag. "It's my day off, and I don't want this to get cold, so I'll stay. For now."

Her gaze is steely, but there is a curve to her lips that tells me the icy walls around her heart are warming, and I pray all is not lost.

We order the chips and guacamole, and the three salsas since I'm curious about them, and once those are demolished, Charlie eats her tacos as I inhale my burritos.

"Do you eat that much every meal?" she asks as I finish the second one.

I nod, my mouth too full to answer verbally.

Charlie's eyes travel down my body. "Where does it all go?"

Her words don't make sense. "Right here, of course," I say, patting my belly.

The laughter that escapes her is wild and loud, and I revel in it. Her shoulders shake with mirth and tears stream down her darkening cheeks, and these are tears I'm proud to take credit for. I don't understand why my words are so humorous, but I don't care, as long as my mate remains this carefree.

"Tell me more about Nia," I say. "She is a brilliant child. You must be very proud."

Her expression goes from gleeful to somber, and I can't figure out why. "Yeah, she's the best thing that's ever happened to me."

My shoulders sag with the guilt of the way I treated her, "leaving her on read" as Sam would put it. Charlie deserved more from me. "Can I apologize once more for—"

"Don't worry about it," she says, cutting me off. "We're all good, Zev. Let's just enjoy the day."

She pours the last of the pitcher into her glass, and I order another one.

"Uh-oh, this is a bad idea," she mutters quietly.

If she's having a bad time, I don't want to keep her here, but I don't think that's the case. Still, I want to be sure. "Would you prefer to leave?"

She looks at the surrounding tables, most still empty, and starts fiddling with one of her long, blonde braids in a way that makes her appear shy all of a sudden. "No, not yet."

She is ours. She forgives us, my draxilio purrs.

I don't know if she forgives us, but I agree, this is progress.

The second pitcher disappears quicker than the first, and with our plates now empty and cleared from the table, there is nothing to slow down our consumption. We speak of music, mostly songs that captured a particular phase of life, songs that helped us move on from one thing to the next, and specific talents—vocal and instrumental—that aren't widely appreciated enough.

After the third pitcher arrives, the alcohol starts taking effect. As a draxilio, it requires a much larger amount of alcohol to achieve a state of drunkenness, and for the first time since arriving on Earth, I think I've reached it.

All I hear is the clinking of glasses and Charlie's melodic giggles. The smell of lime and tequila fills the air, but beneath it, Charlie's warm scent is present and welcome. Her face, her magnificently beautiful face, starts to blur before me. The last thing I remember is her taking my hand and saying we should go for a walk. Then there is nothing. Only her touch.

Then there is pain. Pain and thirst and more pain.

I don't know what happened, but clearly the decision to order a third pitcher was a bad one.

Groaning, I roll onto my side and reach for my phone. It's not on the corner of my nightstand where it usually is.

Curious.

Opening my eyes is a chore, but eventually, I do and am extremely confused by what I see.

This is not my nightstand.

This is not my room.

I feel my pants and shoes still on my body as I turn to my left and find Charlie fast asleep beside me, snoring loudly, and also fully clothed.

A quick glance at my arm tells me I have unmasked while asleep, but if Charlie had noticed my blue skin and tall black horns, I assume her sleep wouldn't be so peaceful. She would've most likely run out of here screaming. To prevent that from happening now, I quickly mask; my horns receding into my skull and my blue scales fading to the pasty human skin I wear whenever I leave the house.

The change in my skin color reveals a message written on the back of my hand, in what looks like black permanent marker.

JUST MARRIED.

"Just married?" I whisper to myself.

Oh no.

No, it can't be.

This can't be true. It has to be some kind of joke. If only I could confirm this with Charlie, I'm sure we'd share a riotous laugh, and my fears would be quelled.

Carefully, I climb out of bed, or off the bed, rather, since I fell asleep on top of the comforter with my shoes on, and silently creep to Charlie's side of the bed. I don't know what I'm looking for. Perhaps proof that this is just a silly game we played after too many margaritas.

My stomach sinks at the sight of *JUST MARRIED* written on the back of her hand as well, and though I have no memory of anything after the arrival of that third pitcher, deep within my gut, I know this is no game.

I pace across the room for a moment, unsure of what to do. Then I catch sight of myself in the mirror and notice my eyes. Peering in closer, I try to remove the contacts, but they're already gone.

But my eyes are no longer red. That can only mean one thing.

Charlie accepted me as her mate—my flightless form and the fire-breathing beast I rarely let out.

She accepted us! My draxilio squeals inside me. *She is truly ours now!*

But...how? Did I tell her? How did she react?

My draxilio grows quiet. *I don't know. I can't remember.*

Well, what the fuck am I supposed to do with that?

There's no way she could accept me without me explicitly telling her I'm a dragon shifter, right? This is not something Luka, Axil, or Mylo have dealt with, so I'm not sure even they would have the answers. But if Charlie doesn't remember me telling her, I can't exactly do it now.

"Good morning, Charlie. You married a dragon. That's not a deal-breaker, is it?"

No, I can't say that.

Confused and disoriented, I do the only thing I can.

I run.

CHAPTER 9

CHARLIE

*M*y head feels like it's been run over by a snowplow. Why the fuck did we order that third pitcher of margaritas? Even the second pitcher was a bad idea. I don't remember drinking from the third pitcher, but the way my brain is throbbing like a stubbed toe, I wouldn't be surprised if I skipped the glass and poured the entire pitcher directly into my mouth.

It's hot in here. Too fucking hot.

I go to kick the blankets off, but nothing happens. When I look down, there are no blankets on top of me, and one of my shoes is still on. In what world would I kick off one shoe and not the other? And what kind of bumpkin goes to bed in their outside clothes?

Gross.

Wait, this isn't my room. Where the hell am I?

Rubbing the sleep from my eyes, I look around and realize this must be a cheap motel. My heart stops as I peer into the small, adjoined bathroom, and I let out a deep breath when I find it empty. Thank goodness I didn't wake up next to some creep.

That wouldn't make sense anyway, since I was with Zev.

Zev! Where is he? Did we end up here together?

I don't remember even leaving the restaurant.

The pounding of my head gets louder, and my palms start to sweat as I attempt to put the pieces of the puzzle together.

Here's what I know for sure: I saw Zev at Pollo Palace and lost my shit. He apologized for ghosting me and offered to buy me a drink. I said yes. We drank. A lot. We also ate a lot. My stomach still hurts from laughing. We laughed for hours. I don't remember what we talked about, but I remember having an absolute blast.

At one point, I said it was a bad idea to keep drinking, and when he asked me if I wanted to leave, I said no. That was the truth. Nothing short of a medical emergency for my dad or Nia could've pulled me away from that table.

Holy shit! Nia.

Frantically, I grab my purse off the floor and dig for my phone. It's only seven in the morning, but I have three missed calls from Dad, and a text telling me that Nia is sound asleep and he hopes I'm out with friends.

That's somewhat of a relief, but it still doesn't explain what happened last night. I call Zev, but his voicemail kicks on after four rings, so I hang up.

I get to my feet and race into the bathroom. Not knowing what else to do, or how to uncover these lost memories, I splash water on my face and stare at my reflection, hoping it'll all come back to me. I woke up fully clothed, so clearly nothing sexual occurred, not even any solo fun. Booking a motel room for one night in the middle of town doesn't make sense, and I have no idea why I would do that, but by the state of the paint and decor, it seems like it didn't cost much money.

I pull up my banking app and see my checking account has the same amount it had yesterday, so that's good, but that means someone else paid for the room. It had to be Zev, but since he's not answering the phone, I can't confirm it.

First things first, I need coffee, and I need it now.

Pulling my braids back into a loose bun, I throw on my hoodie and my sunglasses and enter the land of the living. I keep my head down as I stumble across the motel parking lot toward the first coffee shop I see, Common Grounds.

I order a large caramel latte with whip and wait by the big window facing the corner of Tremont Street and Route 3. Now I know where I am. Pollo Palace is a couple blocks down on Tremont, and I could walk there from here in about six minutes. So if Zev and I left Pollo Palace, it's not unthinkable that we would end up at the motel, though I'm still not sure why. We clearly didn't hook up, right?

"There she is. How was the honeymoon?" Caitlyn hollers across the shop, stopping my heart completely.

Why does that question chill me to the bone? I let out a nervous laugh, then walk/run toward her. "I'm sorry, what did you just say?"

"That bad, eh?"

"No. I mean, what are you talking about?"

She grabs my left hand and turns it over, showing me the words "JUST MARRIED" written in all caps and black ink across the back.

I stare at it, trying to make sense of what I'm seeing. "What in the *what*?"

"You seriously don't remember? Damn, I knew you guys were drunk, but I didn't think you were *that* drunk."

"Caitlyn," I grunt, pressing my thumb into the spot over my left eye that's throbbing so hard, I can barely stand, "explain. I'm begging you."

Caitlyn orders her coffee, a large drip with a shot of peppermint, and pulls me back toward the big window. "You and Zev got married last night," she says quietly. "I officiated."

"Why would we get married?" I ask, knowing she probably doesn't have the answer beyond us just being that drunk, but it doesn't make sense to me. Then I realize how mad I am at Caitlyn for letting it happen. "Why would you officiate when we were clearly drunk off our asses?"

She sighs impatiently. "Ugh, Jesus, I'm really going to have to walk you through this, aren't I? Fine."

The barista calls my name, and I remove the top of my coffee so I can blow on it in order to guzzle it at the first possible opportunity.

"You and Zev were leaving Pollo Palace as I was picking up my lunch. You told me you were heading to city hall because you wanted to get married. I told you I was the only one who could approve your marriage license, as town clerk, and you both started cheering. So you walked back with me, filled out the paperwork, and when I told you I was also an officiant, Zev lifted you above his head like in *Dirty Dancing,* and you thanked me and promised you'd name your child after me."

Spinning. My head is absolutely spinning.

"If you want, you can come back to the office with me and I'll make a copy of your certificate, since, I'm assuming, in your sloppy state, you lost the original?"

She didn't answer my question. "Again, I ask, *why* would you marry us?"

Caitlyn looks around, checking to see if anyone is listening. "You pulled me aside and told me about your baby daddy. About him wanting custody. I married you because a—having a husband will give you a better shot at maintaining sole custody, and b—have you *seen* your husband? Honey, you get the opportunity to lock a guy like that down, you take it. Frankly, I'm a little offended you haven't thanked me yet."

I can't deny that Zev is a whole-ass meal, and maybe I convinced him to marry me while we were both hammered, but we can't stay married. It's bad enough that this is all my fault, and as soon as Zev realizes what we've done, he's going to want this marriage annulled. Come to think of it, that's probably why I woke up alone. He's probably home right now, wondering how he could've been stupid enough to agree to this.

But the first part of what she said is pulling my focus. "Why do you think I need a husband to maintain custody?" Evan made it sound like if we were standing in front of a judge, the judge would see him as this stable golden boy, and I'd look like some flaky whore, but that can't be true, can it?

"Girl, I know the judges in this town. They're all old white men with traditional values," she explains. "If Evan is as manipulative as you claim, he's going to strut into that courtroom with his wife on his arm and her pregnant belly popping out of her dress, he's going to talk about his achievements in Congress, and he's going to make you look terrible.

"You wanna beat him? You need the judges to see you're a settled, hardworking mom who is giving your daughter everything Evan says he's prepared to give her. Show them that your daughter has everything she needs already."

I can't argue with her logic, but how am I supposed to convince Zev to stick it out through a custody battle?

Maybe I'm overreacting. It's not like I've been served yet. Evan says he wants quality time with her, which could just mean visitation. Although, I'm not inclined to give him that, so if he's prepared to sue me for custody, he probably will. I don't want him within a mile of my daughter. Not even for a supervised visit.

"Zev has a good job, right?" Caitlyn asks, breaking through my stress-cloud of thoughts.

"Um, he was a tattoo artist," I tell her, "but he recently quit."

"Okay, what's he doing now?"

He told me he quit the tattoo place, but he never said what he chose to do instead. "I-I don't know. I think he might be between jobs."

Caitlyn nods, but I notice a slight, almost imperceptible wince. Not a good sign. "But he owns his house, right? He has a mortgage?"

"I think he lives with his brothers. They bought it together. I don't know how many of them still live there. Axil moved in with Vanessa. Mylo and Sam bought the house next door. So, it might just be him and Kyan."

At the mention of Kyan, her eyes light up. "He's the last single one, right? Is he seeing—"

"Caitlyn, please. One thing at a time."

"Right. Sorry." She chews on her perfectly manicured red thumbnail for a moment. "Does he have money?"

"Oh, yes," I tell her, relieved to give her something that might work in my favor. "All of them are wealthy."

"Really? Then why do they still live together?"

I shrug. I've wondered the same myself.

"Well, that's good. Money is the key to everything, so as long as he can show some bank statements to the judge to prove that you have the means to care for Nia without Evan's help, I'm sure it'll be fine."

She's right. It all comes down to money.

The barista calls Caitlyn's name, and as she grabs her coffee, she threads her arm through mine. "This was fun. Want me to give you a ride back to your car?"

"I disagree on the fun part since, you know, my life is quickly unraveling, and I've just discovered that I have a husband I don't remember acquiring," I say with a weary sigh, "but thank you for your help. I appreciate it."

"Happy to help."

I climb into the passenger side of her olive-green Subaru Outback, and she blasts the Spice Girls on our very quick ride to Pollo Palace. The restaurant is directly across from city hall, and as I go to open the door, I see Evan's rental car in the parking lot, and Evan walking out of the building, striding toward it.

"Fuck, that's him," I whisper to Caitlyn, ducking down in my seat. "Wait, is that..."

"Councilman Vincent? Yep."

There's a third man, an older man, who climbs into Evan's backseat. "Who is that? I don't recognize him."

"That's Judge Cromwell."

"The fuck? Is he allowed to engage in such blatant bribery? Are any of them?"

Caitlyn bursts out laughing. When she sees that I'm not, she stops and clears her throat. "Sorry, I didn't realize that was a serious question."

They drive past us, Evan smiling as he speeds off. I can't let that smug motherfucker take my daughter. I can't.

"Go talk to Zev," Caitlyn urges, her tone softening. "He seems like a good guy. I'm sure he'll help you."

Why would he help me? He has no reason to do so, and staying married to me through a custody battle will only benefit me, and it will seriously inconvenience him. There's no way he'll go for this.

CHAPTER 10

ZEV

"Zevrick Allenwrench Monroe," Sam says with a tsk. "I am disappointed in you."

"That's not my name. Not even close."

"You just ran?" Vanessa shouts. "You left your wife alone in a shitty motel room and ran?"

I don't know where my brothers are, but I wish one of them was home right now.

"What was I supposed to do?" I ask, my hands sweating. My back is sweating. Every inch of me is sweating.

Sam shakes her head disapprovingly before taking a sip of her iced coffee. "Um, not run."

"My eyes are no longer red, see? That means she knows what I am. I told her. I just don't remember telling her, or what her reaction was."

Vanessa leans back in her kitchen stool and rests her feet on the one next to it. "If you can't remember telling her the truth, or the fact that you two, you know, got married, then I doubt she remembers."

"What am I supposed to do then? How do I proceed?" I drop my face on the kitchen counter and wrap my arms around my head. This is awful. It's my fault, and I don't know how to fix it.

"Well, she's probably going to wake up very confused and

hungover. Then she'll want to talk to you, to figure out what the hell happened," Sam says. "Beyond that, I imagine she'll want to get the marriage annulled immediately since it was a drunken mistake."

"But she's my mate. I need to find a way to keep her."

"So what's your plan? To stay married to a woman who may or may not know you're an alien-dragon shifter?" The way Vanessa looks at me tells me that would be a terrible plan.

"No," I reply sheepishly. "That's why I need your help."

The doorbell rings, and I feel the blood drain from my face.

Vanessa pulls up the app on her phone that shows her the footage of our security cameras and the ones around her property. "Yup, it's Charlie."

Not that I needed the confirmation. Her cinnamon-y scent is currently filling my lungs. Without thinking, I race toward my bedroom to hide.

"Zev," Sam loudly whispers. "What the hell?"

I crouch at the edge of the kitchen and clasp my hands together. "Talk to her. Please. Find out if she knows."

"Of course," Vanessa says, just as Sam replies, "What's in it for me?"

What's in it for her? "W-what do you want?"

"You promised me a free tattoo. I know you still have all the equipment in the basement. I'd like to have it done in the next few weeks."

"Fine!" I reply, trying to shout as loudly as possible while still whispering. "Of what?"

Sam stands there thinking as if my mate isn't waiting at the front door. When the doorbell rings a second time, she snaps out of it. "A raven."

"A raven?" Vanessa echoes. "Why a raven?"

"Mylo has been reading me a lot of Edgar Allan Poe lately, so..."

Now? They choose to have this discussion *now*?

"A raven. Yes. Very well," I say, my voice trembling with anticipation. "I promise I will do that."

"Yay," Sam cheers with raised fists, then races toward the front door as I crawl across the hallway carpet into my bedroom, leaving it cracked enough for me to hear their conversation.

"Charlie," they shout, greeting her at the same time.

"Uh, hey," she replies, her voice scratchy as if she's just woken up. "Is Zev home? I kind of need to talk to him."

"Yeah, he came home a little while ago. Seemed pretty beat, so he might be asleep," Vanessa warns. "Did you guys have fun last night?"

"Why, did he say something?" Charlie asks, her tone stiff and nervous.

"Oh, no, no," Sam assures her. "He just said he was out with you. That's all."

They stand there, the three of them, not saying anything for what feels like an excruciatingly long time.

"So..." Vanessa pipes in. "You know what I miss? *Game of Thrones.*"

"Oh, yeah," Sam agrees. "Loved that show."

This is their plan? This, really?

"Um, yeah. I loved it too." Charlie agrees, not nearly as passionately as Sam or Vanessa, but she agrees. I suppose that's a good start.

"Who was your favorite character?" Sam asks Vanessa.

"Hmm, I would have to say..." she trails off, pretending to contemplate her answer. "The dragons. Gotta be the dragons. Weren't they great, Charlie?"

I am so embarrassed for them. This was a mistake, and it's very hard to listen to. Is this how I sound when I speak to people? If so, then I understand why no one sticks around.

"Do you like dragons?" Sam asks.

Charlie chuckles quietly. "I'd love to do a deep dive on *Game of Thrones* with y'all, but maybe some other time? I have to get home soon. Lots to do today. And I really, *really* need to talk to Zev."

"Of course," Vanessa says.

Sam tells Charlie to come inside. "We'll go get him."

They creep down the hall to my room and poke their heads in. "So, we fucked it. We totally fucked it," Vanessa whispers.

"You're screwed," Sam adds, patting me on the back. "Good luck though!"

They turn back and tell Charlie that I'm awake and to come to my room before saying they're heading next door to Vanessa's in order to give us some privacy. It's the only part of this they've done correctly. Nevertheless, I appreciate that they tried.

Charlie shyly approaches and closes the door to my bedroom behind her. I can't help the calm that settles over me at the sight of my mate mere feet from my bed. She's right where she's meant to be, in my home, by my side. Yet I'm terrified that she's about to walk away and never look back.

"Morning, husband," she says with a nervous laugh, immediately followed by a cringe. "Sorry, that was a bad joke." She drops her purse next to my dresser and scrubs a hand down her face. Her braids are falling out of the loose bun at the nape of her neck, there are dark circles beneath her eyes, and she looks as if she might fall asleep while standing.

My mate has never looked more beautiful. "I don't mean to make light of the situation, and obviously, we made some choices last night that seem insane today. We were very drunk and honestly, I don't remember much of what happened after that third pitcher, but this," she shows me the words on her hand, "along with the fact that Caitlyn admitted that she was our officiant—"

"Wait, Caitlyn? The little woman from the Twilight party?"

"Yeah. As the town clerk, she approved our application for a marriage license, and then officiated our...wedding, if you can even call it that."

Her words are like a knife to my chest. I realize a simple ceremony at city hall after consuming far too much alcohol and while wearing jeans and sneakers is no one's idea of a romantic wedding. I hate myself for robbing Charlie of the kind of celebration she deserves. Nia wasn't even there.

Tears pool in Charlie's eyes as she begins speaking at a rapid pace. "Listen, this is my mess. I got us into this, and the reason is so stupid. My ex, Nia's dad, showed up at my house the other day, threatening to seek custody of her so he can use her as a prop for his upcoming campaign. He's a congressman, by the way, and a complete monster.

"Anyway, he was saying all this stuff about how the judge would take one look at me and then him and see him as the more stable parent. He made it seem like he was going to take her away from me, and I guess, I don't know, I was feeling hurt that you blew me off, or it seemed like you blew me off, so when we started drinking, I must've thought the way to keep my child was to find a husband, an-and–"

I take her hand and press her palm against my chest. "Breathe," I tell her. She's talking so fast, and the tears are falling so quickly, that she hasn't taken a breath since she launched into this story.

She nods, and I can tell she wants to do as I say, but her breaths come in short, quick pants as she continues. "Anyway, Caitlyn said I should try to convince you to stay married to me until this whole custody mess is behind me because having a husband will make me look better to the judges of this town, but I can't do that to you. I won't do that to you."

She doesn't realize she's giving us exactly what we want, my drax-ilio points out.

I know, but shh, I send back. *Let her finish.*

A bubble of snot forms at her left nostril, and it might be the most adorable thing I've ever seen. "This is my mess, and I'm going to take care of it. So don't worry, I'll get the paperwork and we can get this annulled right away."

"No."

Charlie stares at me, blinking rapidly with her mouth open wide. "Huh?"

"No," I repeat. "I want us to stay married."

"But why?"

Why? That's complicated. The easy part of this is that I know she's my mate, and that she, Nia, and I are meant to be a family. It's a knowing that runs deeper than information I've learned or any memories I've made. I am fated to be hers, just as she is to be mine. When I look into her eyes, I know these are the eyes I will get lost in every day that follows until my very last day on Earth.

84 | IVY KNOX

However, I only know that because I am draxilio, and despite my genetic mutations, we have fated mates just as every natural-born draxilio from Sufoi. Charlie is human, and their kind is not gifted with the ability to recognize one's mate when they stand before them.

I want to stay married to her because she is mine. I just need to show her that I am hers. This marriage, sham or not, gives me time to prove my worth to her.

My handlers reminded me often that, to them, I'm useless, and that my destiny is to accomplish nothing of note. To merely take up space and get in the way of those who were meant to leave impressive legacies in their wake.

But I'm not useless, and I will make sure Charlie sees that. As her husband, I have the opportunity to protect her from this vile ex of hers who threatens to steal Nia from her. I can protect Nia as well and give her a safe environment in which to grow into the incredible person she is meant to become. To Charlie, it may seem like I'm making a sacrifice by agreeing to remain married, but she's wrong. Finding one's mate, forming that bond, and creating a family together is the highest honor bestowed upon a draxilio.

It doesn't happen for everyone, and I certainly didn't believe it would for me, but Charlie's very existence is proof that I, too, am worthy of this honor. And I would die before I let her and Nia down.

"This man, this ex," I grit, my fists clenching at the mere mention of him, "he's evil, yes? You don't trust him around Nia?"

"Evil, yes. Big time. He's a liar and a narcissist, and he's abusive—"

My draxilio begs for release. *Kill. Kill, kill. Find and kill.*

"Abusive?" I ask, pushing him back down. "He abused you?"

I have enough experience to know that when someone willingly causes harm to another living creature, they don't stop. It becomes a hunger they continue to feed, either on bigger, stronger creatures, or on the very same one, over and over, until their victim is broken beyond repair.

The only reason my handlers stopped abusing me is because I left the planet. Had I stayed, I'd have fresh wounds across my back every day, scar tissue transforming more of my flesh into hardened, uneven marks that will never fade.

Nia will not suffer the same fate. If this man hurt Charlie, he will hurt others, if he hasn't already.

Charlie nods. "When I found out I was pregnant, I ran. I didn't want him anywhere near my daughter." Her voice gets quiet. "I've been running ever since."

I pull her into my arms and when I feel her return my embrace, I gently kiss her hair. "You don't need to run anymore. We'll stay married, and I'll help you defeat this ex. You won't lose custody of Nia. I promise."

She pulls back to look at me. "I don't understand. Why would you do this?"

I offer the truth. Well, a truth. "I don't like bullies, Charlie. We aren't going to let this one win."

A fresh set of tears fall from her eyes, and she sags against me, pressing her head hard into my chest as I hold her in my arms.

Finally, my draxilio sighs. *She is home.*

Time to make this a home she never wishes to flee, I send back.

Now that we've agreed to stay married, I must get to work on making Charlie fall in love with me. There's no time to spare. "We should go on a date. A real first date. Tonight, perhaps?" Reluctantly, I release Charlie as my mind fills with ideas and tasks that need to be completed. "And you should move in. You and Nia. You'll have your own bedroom, of course, if you prefer, and there's a spare room we've been using as an office, but I can quickly turn that into a bedroom for Nia. She likes dragons, yes? I remember her saying she likes dragons." I turn to face a very bewildered Charlie. "How quickly can you pack your things?"

CHAPTER 11

CHARLIE

*W*hat have I done? Is this the right move? Zev is extremely eager to remain married, which is great. It'll help me with the custody drama, but wow. He's practically buzzing as he paces around his room discussing our immediate future. When I was talking to Caitlyn about trying to stay married to Zev, I didn't realize all the ways my life would change, or how soon.

When I showed up at his house, I had every intention of bribing him to play my husband for the next couple months. Free books, sexual favors, and a lifetime supply of home-cooked meals were all on the table. But when I was standing in front of him with his messy man bun, his kind, different-colored eyes—one blue, one green—and his open expression, as if his heart is exposed for the taking, I just couldn't pressure him that way. He deserves better.

Yet here he is, offering to stay married so I can keep my kid.

I owe him my life.

The cynical part of me worries there's a catch. Some dark secret that hasn't come out. Like, maybe he's really into close-up magic, or has an extensive gun collection in the basement, or something.

Build your village. Find your people and lean on them.

My dad's voice is loud and clear in my head. I trust Zev. I'm not sure why, but I do. When he talked about not letting bullies win, his eyes held pain. I had a feeling, given how awkward he can be, that he's been bullied in the past, but it's clear there's more to it than that. I won't push him to share it because it's none of my business, but I'm relieved to have someone on my side.

Why couldn't my dad show up for me like that?

"Tonight?" I ask, answering his first question of about a hundred. "Sure, I'd love to go on a date tonight. We don't have to move in together though. That seems a little fast."

"Oh," he says, his face falling. "But won't you need to use this as your primary address? Or would you prefer to remain at your father's house?"

No, I definitely can't do that. How would it look for a married couple to be living in separate houses? Plus, I need to be out of my dad's place soon anyway, and I haven't found anything affordable around here. Fuck, I guess this is as good a time as any to move out. Don't I need everything he's offering?

"You're right," I tell Zev. "And I'd love to go out. Grab some dinner, maybe? I need to go home and spend the day with Nia, and I'll check with Dad to make sure he can watch her tonight."

He smiles, and it's like a light inside him has turned on. The way he glows when he's happy is mesmerizing. "That's perfect. I'll take care of everything, Charlie. Don't worry."

My stomach leaps, and suddenly it's hard to stand still. I love the way he says my name with that deep, velvety growl of his. By the time he gets to the "lie" in my name, I get a peek at the tip of his tongue pressed against his top teeth, and every time, I wonder what it would feel like to have that tongue against my skin. Those teeth nipping at my neck.

"May I pick you up at seven?"

"You may."

He steps forward and his arms shoot out as if he wants to pull me back in for another hug. Then, suddenly, his cheeks turn bright red, and he drops his arms to his sides before offering one hand to shake.

I laugh at his shyness, and I'm slightly annoyed I didn't get to kiss my new husband, but there's plenty of time for that later.

By the time I pull my car into the driveway, I'm bouncing with energy. It's only nine-thirty, so I have the whole day to spend with my baby girl. "Hello, family," I call out. "Who wants to help me take out my braids?"

Nia and Dad both groan from the kitchen as I throw the door closed behind me.

"Come on," I plead. "With the three of us, it should only take an hour...maybe two."

"First of all, where have you been?" Dad says with a look of mock irritation. "You stay out all night and then the first thing I hear is that you need help taking out your braids?"

Where do I even begin? "I had a, uh, a fun night. Eventful, but fun."

"Eventful?" Dad asks.

Shit. I shouldn't have used that word. I should've said, *it was fun and perfectly safe, and I didn't drunkenly marry anyone.*

"No, not eventful. Not really. It was great. Nice to cut loose."

He leans down and kisses my cheek as I pass him. "That's good, honey. Glad you had fun. You were due."

"Why are you taking your braids out?" Nia asks as she rips the crust off her toast.

I pour myself some orange juice, grab a muffin from the plastic container, and sit next to Nia. "Because I've had them in for six weeks, and I'm ready for them to come out." I clear my throat. "Also... because I have a date."

They look at each other and gasp. "A date?"

"With who?" Nia asks.

"Whom," my dad corrects.

Nia's wide smile shrinks. "That man from dinner the other night?"

Ugh. The memory of him in this house will haunt me for the rest of my days. "No, it's with the man from the library. Zev. Remember Nia? You met him."

"The pretty tiger man!" she shouts with glee. "I like him."

Thank god because this plan is not going to work without Nia. "Me too, baby. Me too." I turn to Dad. "Do you mind watching her tonight for a bit?"

"Of course I don't mind," he barks out with enthusiasm, poking me with his elbow. "I told you to go build your village and here you are doing it."

"Thank you. He's picking me up at seven, but we shouldn't be out too late."

"Eh, stay out late if you want. Me and the baby will be here watching TV."

Nia puts on a mean mug. "I'm not a baby."

Dad sucks in a breath. "Since when?"

"I wanna watch *The Floor Is Lava*," she says, crossing her arms.

"Nope. Nope, nope. We've seen too much of that lately. How about *The Golden Girls?*"

"Adventure Time," Nia counters.

Dad groans. *"The Great British Baking Show*, and that's my final offer."

Nia chews her toast as she stares Dad down. "Okay."

"Ha-ha!" Dad cheers. "See? Now that's how you negotiate."

The three of us finish our breakfast, and I drag one of the kitchen chairs into the center of the living room. Placing a foldable TV tray next to me, I lay out my brush, my comb, and a pair of scissors, and I get to work cutting the bottom four inches of my braids off. I'm careful not to cut too high, as I don't want to hit my natural hair. Once the braids are cut, Dad and Nia stand behind me, unraveling them one by one while I pick them out.

We take breaks when Nia has to pee or wants a snack, and when Dad wants coffee or to watch the news for a bit. It ends up taking close to three hours, but when it's finally done, I feel like I've lost forty pounds from the neck up. I give Nia three dollars for helping, and my dad a kiss on the cheek. He rolls his eyes, pretending to be mad about the lack of compensation, but then giggles as he sits in his chair with a contented sigh.

I make us ham and cheese sandwiches for lunch, with ruffled chips and pickles on the side, and as Dad washes the dishes, Nia yawns and throws herself on the love seat.

"Sleepy?" I ask, rubbing her back. "Want to take a nap with me?"

She opens her arms wide, and I carry her upstairs. "Going to take a nap, Dad."

"Okay, ladies. Get that beauty rest."

We climb onto my bed and Nia settles herself in the middle. I tuck myself around her and pile the blankets high on top of us. The way she nuzzles against my shoulder and into my neck reminds me of when she was a baby. Just constantly attaching herself to me. She could never get close enough. I miss that closeness, that desire to stay physically connected. Throughout her five years on this Earth, it's been me and her.

It's a blessing to watch her grow and become this independent, strong girl. She needs to be tough for all the hurdles she'll face in life, and I know she will be. But, man, I can't imagine having to spend an entire twenty-four hours without her. If Evan gets custody, I'm not sure how I'll survive those days. Not being able to picture where she is or the bed she'll be sleeping in. Not knowing if she feels safe, or if Evan is giving her the love and support she needs.

He's not capable of giving her that because he doesn't have it to give in the first place. He's got a wife and a high-profile job, and he wears expensive suits, but beyond that? There's nothing. If it doesn't serve him or his political aspirations, he doesn't care about it, and Nia shouldn't be exposed to someone with such an empty heart, especially if that someone is her father.

I fall asleep to the sound of her steady breaths and the warmth of her small body wrapped around mine.

When I wake, it's a quarter to four, and I peel myself away from Nia so I can wash my hair. I find Nia poking through my closet when I come out of the shower. "Whatcha doin', cupcake?"

"Looking at your clothes," she says with a hopeless exhale that makes me feel like I need to go shopping. "What are you gonna wear?"

"I don't know. What do you think I should wear?"

She pulls three dresses off their hangers and gently lays them out on the bed. I model each of them for her, and her feedback is far too harsh for my delicate state, but we end up going with a short-sleeved satin midi wrap dress in a deep burgundy color and black ankle booties. I pair it with a cropped faux-leather moto jacket and a sequined black clutch.

Once my hair and makeup are done, I put the outfit on and stroll down the hall into the living room like it's a runway.

"Well?" I ask, giving my dad and Nia a spin.

Nia's hands are covering her mouth, and behind those hands, I see a smile. "So pretty, Mommy."

"Aww, thank you, baby."

"Look at you," Dad says with a warm, loving expression that reminds me of how he looked at me on prom night. "My daughter. Come here."

I run into his outstretched arms, and we share a swaying hug around the living room carpet.

The knock at the door has me chewing on the inside of my cheek, nerves making me shake. Dad goes to answer it, but I know he's just going to give Zev a hard time, so I step in front of him and throw the door open.

Zev is dressed in a dark gray suit that looks a smidge too big around the shoulders, but the white shirt beneath, the pants, and the gray striped tie look like they were custom-made just for his spectacular body. The combination of the suit and the tattoos that peek out from his sleeves, covering his hands, has me squeezing my thighs together. I want those hands all over me.

His light brown hair is smoothed back in a neat bun, and he has a breathtaking bouquet of flowers in his grip.

After devouring him with my eyes from the neck down, my gaze lifts to his face, and he's looking at me like I'm the sun, and he's seeing me for the first time. "You took out your braids," he says, his voice husky and thick with emotion he's trying to conceal.

"I did," I reply, suddenly feeling a little shy. I love my braids. Maybe I should've left them in? "What do you think?"

"I think..." he starts, his different-colored eyes slowly moving over my face and hair, but not in a scrutinizing way. It feels more like a caress. "I think you're the most beautiful thing I have ever seen."

"That's the correct answer," Dad pipes in.

Damn. I forgot there were other people here. "Dad, this is Zev. Zev, this is my father, Darius."

Dad clears his throat and extends his hand. "Nice to meet you, son."

Son? Dad has never referred to any of my boyfriends in such an intimate way. Though I shouldn't be too surprised. Zev radiates good vibes, and my dad probably senses that he's not a total asshole.

Nia peeks her head out from behind me and waves.

"And you remember my daughter, Nia?"

"Of course I do," Zev replies, reaching into the pocket of his blazer. "I brought you a box of crayons. They're yours to use or break. Up to you."

"You will not break them," I tell her. "You hear me?"

She runs off, crayons in hand, giggling wildly. I'm definitely coming home to broken crayons all over the floor.

I hand Dad my bouquet, and he promises to cut the ends and put them in water. Zev offers his arm, and guides me to the car, opening and closing my door for me. It sucks that basic manners are so impressive, but I can't lie, it makes me feel like a queen.

On the drive to Manchester, Zev tells me about the restaurant. It's a pop-up dining experience, and he's skeptical, but Mylo told him it's supposed to be the fanciest place in the state with the most expensive menu items. "I probably shouldn't have mentioned the price," he mutters quietly. "That's not a sexy date topic. My apologies. I'd like to pay for your meal, and the food is reasonably priced, and I don't expect anything in return."

Now he's rambling because he's nervous. It's adorable.

"Should you decide you like the meal, and wish to thank me at the end of the evening with a kiss, I'll be delighted, but you should know that I don't expect even that—"

"Zev, it's okay," I tell him, putting a hand on his arm. "I don't care if the food sucks and is ridiculously overpriced. No matter what, I'm kissing you tonight."

I watch his throat work as he swallows, and it blows my mind that this man is mine. Mine! All mine. My luck has famously been shit, but maybe it's finally starting to turn around.

The restaurant only has six tables, and all are occupied but ours. I expect to be handed a menu when we're seated, but the server tells us that the first course of seven will be coming out shortly, and that there's a wine pairing for each course.

We clink our glasses when the wine arrives, a medium-bodied Grenache with hints of coffee and black currant. Unable to resist, I say, "To my husband."

He laughs, his chin dipping in embarrassment at the absurdity of our situation. "To my wife."

When the first course arrives, Zev and I share a wary but amused glance. The thing on my plate looks like bubbles coming out of a miniature eggroll on a bed of spinach and pink cream. It's weird, but I try not to judge a book by its cover, so I use my fork to break up the eggroll and scoop a bubble onto the end. Zev follows my lead.

It's about a thousand degrees, but even if it weren't, the eggroll tastes like deep-fried ass, and the bubble tastes like mint. But deep-fried ass covered in mint is still deep-fried ass. I don't spit it out, even though it's so hot that I'm tempted to, but I want the date to go well, so I wash it down with wine and spend the next few minutes waving a hand in front of my charred tongue.

"I did not like that," Zev says, blowing out a breath.

"I'm sure the next one will be better," I assure him, and I'm really hoping I'm right.

Turns out, I'm wrong. The next course is so much worse. The wine is a dry rosé with notes of lavender, which is fine, but the dish is some kind of mushroom foam sitting atop a pile of black fuzz, and the base looks like a saltine cracker. The best way to describe the flavor would be how I feel when I've been on hold for ten-plus minutes.

"Please tell me you didn't pay a hundred dollars for this disgusting meal," I whisper to Zev.

He looks around sheepishly. "I didn't."

A sigh of relief whooshes out of me.

"I paid three hundred."

"Three hundred?" I reply much too loudly. Everyone else, including the servers, gives me a nasty look. "Zev, I'm sorry. I know you wanted to take me to a fancy place, but I'd rather eat a cheeseburger off the floor of a men's restroom."

His sip of wine sprays all over his plate as he laughs, then he hides behind his cloth napkin as he wipes the rosé off his tie.

"This place isn't really me, and it doesn't seem like it's you either."

He nods, dropping his napkin on his plate. "You're right. It's not. Let's go somewhere else."

Pulling out his wallet, he drops three hundred-dollar bills on the table and says, "Hey, thanks," to the nearest server, and gets to his feet. A man who tips well even when the food is inedible? That's incredibly sexy. My nipples pebble beneath my dress, and I have to stifle the moan that threatens to escape when I feel his hand on the small of my back as he guides me out of the restaurant.

The ride back home is quick, and when he pulls off at the Concord exit, I ask him where he's taking me.

"Do you like Five Guys? You got me in the mood for a cheeseburger."

"Did you not hear the rest of my sentence?" I was providing a visual that I thought would thoroughly disgust him.

"I didn't hear anything after *cheeseburger*, I'm afraid," he says with a deep, husky laugh that sends a jolt of electricity down my spine and straight to my clit.

We each order a cheeseburger, fries, and a salted caramel milkshake then I tell him we should eat at this spot I know overlooking the river. I show him where to go, and I'm thrilled when we pull into the spot and there's no one else around. I plan on eating my burger and tackling this man.

"Wow, look at the stars," he says between fries. He leans forward, practically pressing his forehead against the windshield in awe. "They're so clear tonight."

I nod, no longer hungry. Not for food anyway. "I love it here."

Zev ate his three burritos from Pollo Palace in record time, but he's taking forever and a day to finish his cheeseburger, and it's driving me mad.

However, I'm not sure what to do when he does finish. It's been a long time since I've had sex. Like, my-hymen-might've-grown-back-long-and-decades since I did it in a car. Should I hold his hand first? Or just grab him by the back of the head and pull him toward my lips?

I feel like I'm giving off a touch-me vibe, but maybe I'm not being obvious. Even if I were being obvious, is Zev the type of man to notice? I wouldn't describe him as oblivious, per se, he just might not pick up on certain cues.

He lets out a contented "ahhh" when he finishes his milkshake, and normally that sound would annoy me, but because it's Zev, it doesn't. I find it cute that he felt it necessary to signify the end of a meal with a sound effect.

Or maybe I'm just that horned up and being annoyed would waste too much time. Who knows?

"Hey," I say in my best attempt to sound seductive. I grab his hand and draw circles on his palm with my thumb. "I had fun tonight."

He shoots me a boyish half-grin that makes him look like a Disney prince. "Is the night over already?"

Yes, an opening. "I hope not." I pull him toward me, and he follows my lead. Inching closer, I lose myself in those smoldering eyes. Fuck, he's so pretty. The distance closes between us, and I stop. I want him to come the rest of the way. "I wish I could remember if we've already had our first kiss," I tell him.

He snickers and brushes his pointer finger across his eyebrow. It shouldn't look hot, such a simple move like that, but it does. "I suppose it doesn't matter," he says, gently cupping my cheek. "You can have a thousand firsts, but you won't remember all of them or even most of them." I lean into his touch, closing my eyes as he runs the pad of his thumb across my bottom lip. "I can't speak for you, Charlie..."

God, the way he says my name. My panties are absolutely soaked.

He leans closer, our lips almost touching. "But I know I will never forget *this* kiss."

"Why's that?" I ask, breathless.

"Because there are no lips…" he says, leaning in and pressing his lips against mine.

It's a gentle kiss, but filled with yearning, and he breaks it far earlier than I would like.

"Quite like yours," he finishes. "Not in the entire fucking universe."

A needy whimper escapes me. I can't help it. I didn't expect the compliment, or the cursing, or for a man with such calloused hands to have lips that are so soft and supple. He starts to pull back, giving me that same boyish grin, but I don't let him get away. I grab the lapels of his blazer and tug him toward me, slamming my mouth against his.

Very quickly, we become two pairs of frenzied hands and two bodies that can't get close enough. We tear at each other's clothes, and I try to wiggle my way into his lap, but suddenly, he stops me.

"Wait," he pants. "We shouldn't."

I'm sorry, what now? "Why not?"

He doesn't say anything, just looks around the car like a good excuse is written on the sunroof.

"I mean, we are married," I joke. "And it's been a while since I've had car sex, but I think if you slide your seat back a little more—"

"I've never done this before." His words are rushed, and once they're out, he drops his head against the window and pinches his eyes closed.

Can this man, this absolute god of a man, truly be a virgin? No, that can't be possible. "You've never done it in a car before or…"

"Never in a car," he mutters as his gaze drops to his empty milkshake. "Never in a bed, never anywhere."

"Okay," I say, not knowing what the fuck else to say. "Um, is it something you'd like to do at some point?" Who knows, maybe he's stayed a virgin this long because he wants to remain one. Maybe penetrative sex isn't his thing. That's fine. Part of me wishes we had this discussion and established sexual boundaries before we became legally bound to one another, but fine. This is fine.

"Of course," he says, his expression tormented. "I want nothing more than to do this with you, right here and now."

I don't understand the problem. "So…"

"I worry that I won't be good at it," he whispers. My heart forms a deep crack down the center at the sight of such raw vulnerability. "I want to be able to please you. I want to know exactly where to touch you to make you scream, to make your entire body quiver with need. When I put my mouth or my tongue on your skin, Charlie, I want it to light you up from the inside. My greatest fear is that when I do, you'll feel nothing."

Well, fuck. Just his words got me three steps closer. We could give it a go, and it might be good, or it might be bad. First times can be that way. It wouldn't matter much to me because I'm patient, and I know a couple has to give it a few college tries before they learn each other's bodies. I hate to see Zev this anxious about it though. If he's this worried, he's not going to enjoy it, and that I will not stand for.

My core clenches as an idea pops into my head that I think will resolve this entire problem. "Wanna watch me?"

"Watch…you? What do you mean?"

"Okay, stay there. Right where you are." I move my seat back, shimmy out of my jacket, unhook my bra and pull it out through my sleeve, then hike the bottom of my dress above my knees. "I'm going to show you exactly how I like to be touched, and all you have to do is watch."

"You would do that?" he asks, swallowing hard. "You'd let me watch you?"

It might not be every woman's bag, but I don't mind an audience. Not just any audience, of course. It has to be someone I trust, and under the right circumstances. More importantly, Zev seems extremely eager to watch me, and if this is how he gets more comfortable with the idea of sex, I'm all for it. "Absolutely. But I do have one rule."

His smile goes from boyish to wolfish, and I can already tell I'm not going to last very long. "Which is?"

"You can't touch me. At some point, you might want to, but you can't. You have to sit there and just watch, from start to finish. Got it?"

He bites his lip, and his face twists into an expression that makes it clear he's regretting his choice already. "Got it. I will not touch you. I promise."

It's our first date and I'm about to masturbate in front of him. It sounds as crazy as it feels, but when he promises me he won't touch me, I believe him.

Leaning back in my seat, I loosen the tie at the front of my dress just enough to let my breasts fall naturally. I spread my legs as wide as they'll go and lift my dress higher until he can see the black lacy swirls of my boy shorts. Arching against my own touch, I circle my nipple slowly, never dropping my gaze from his, plucking it until it hardens beneath the fabric.

His eyes follow my hand, the pink tip of his tongue darting out to wet his lip as I pull on the tip of my breast, his breath coming out in shallow gusts.

Giving the same attention to my other breast, I slowly untie the front of my dress and open it wide. He gasps at the sight and his pupils dilate. Normally, I might prefer a more flattering angle to expose my rolls and cellulite than the front seat of a car, but Zev is looking at me like he wants to devour me in a single bite, so I don't give it a second thought. Fuck it. I love my body, and it seems he does too.

Moving my hand down, he bites into his knuckle when I reach my lower stomach. "There," he groans, his nails digging into the cushion of his seat. "Squeeze it for me."

"Yeah?" I ask, surprised by the request.

He nods, his gaze turning absolutely feral when my fingers sink into my skin.

"Like this?" I ask, using both hands to grip and massage the generous flesh around my middle.

"Fuck," he grits, frantically loosening his tie. "You're so beautiful."

I continue traversing my body with my hand and move it lower, slipping it beneath my underwear. I'm not surprised to discover that my folds and inner thighs are soaked, and I use the moisture to swipe across my swollen clit.

"I can't see you," he whispers, anguished. "Please. Let me see you."

Quickly, I shove my panties down my legs and kick them off before resuming my performance.

He sucks in a breath when I reveal my pussy to him, clenching his fists in an obvious attempt to keep from reaching for me.

"No touching," I remind him.

He nods, cracking his knuckles, keeping his hands busy.

Then I close my eyes and go for it. Dipping a finger inside to coat it with slickness, I pull back out and focus my attention on my clit. Circling it, swiping across it quickly, and changing directions as I chase my release. I don't pay attention to what Zev is doing. Though this is for him, I want to enjoy this too. That's kind of the whole point. Angling myself a little more toward him so he gets a clear view, I move my hand faster, my back arching as my thighs start to shake.

I hear "*Fuck*, Charlie," but the voice is distant. He could be on the other side of the river for all I know. My eyes roll back as my body shatters from within. I let out moan after moan until my body sags against the seat, a spent puddle in a very nice dress.

When I open my eyes, the first thing I notice is teeth marks on Zev's headrest. Was watching me so enjoyable for him that he actually bit into his damn seat? I put on a better show than I thought.

Pulling my dress closed and tying it back up, I clear my throat and say, "So, that's how it's done."

CHAPTER 12

ZEV

I can't get my mind to stray from Charlie. The roll of her hips against her hand as she moaned, the way the delicate lips of her cunt glistened with her come, the way her breasts bounced harder the more erratic her movements became…I've jerked myself off more than a dozen times in the last forty-eight hours just to the memory of it all.

The scent of her still lingers on my tie. It couldn't have been more than a handful of seconds, just during that first kiss, but it was the only time our bodies were pressed against each other, and in that time, she covered my tie in that warm cinnamon ambrosia, and I've kept it within an arm's reach ever since, for whenever I need to breathe her in.

She is glorious, my mate. I'm not sure how such luck came my way, but I won't take it for granted.

When I haven't been jerking my cock, I've been busy preparing the bedrooms that will be Nia's and Charlie's. I'm hoping Charlie will quickly discover that her rightful place is in my bed with me, but until she does, she can slumber in Luka's old bedroom down the hall, and Nia can have the office that sits between my room and Charlie's.

Nia's room has been painted a soft teal shade, and most of the furniture has been delivered and assembled. I didn't ask Charlie to move anything from her dad's house, as I know Nia will still spend an occasional night there, so every item in this room is brand new. I hope Nia likes what I've chosen. Sam and Mylo helped me select every detail. She has a twin bed with a built-in nightstand, a full toy box, a desk to do her homework, shelves overflowing with books, a small arts and crafts table, and a dresser. I even got her a comforter with pink dragons on it, complete with dragon-shaped throw pillows.

"Charlie and Nia will be here soon for our family date," I tell Axil and Kyan. "Is there anything else that needs to be moved?"

"Make room in that corner for her rocking chair," Axil grunts.

"What rocking chair?" I don't remember ordering a rocking chair.

He wipes his hands with a rag. "The one I'm going to make for her. It will take about a month, so don't put anything else in that corner in the meantime."

He's a mostly silent brute, but his heart may be the softest among us. "Thank you, brother."

Kyan rubs his palms together. "I'm looking forward to this house not being so quiet."

We both look at Kyan as if someone has taken over his mind.

"You are?" Axil asks.

He puts his hands on his slim waist. "Yes. With all of you going off and getting mated, it's been rather boring around here. I've grown tired of it, and I'm pleased to see that will soon change."

Kyan sharing something heartfelt and emotional? How strange. "Are you okay?"

Axil puts a hand on his shoulder. "Have you been lonely?"

Seeing Kyan uncomfortable is always a good time. "Perhaps the vengeful Monroe brother is finally ready to take a mate."

"How dare you," Kyan says with a glare. "Humans are repulsive. All of their natural odors, and even worse, their unnatural odors! Why must they use so many products to cover the way they smell? It makes it so much worse."

"Very well, you shall be alone forever," Axil mutters with a dismissive wave. "It happened for each of us, but I'm sure it won't happen for you."

Kyan grumbles something under his breath as he stomps out of the room.

Axil says he needs to return to Vanessa as she's been feeling unwell, and I thank him as he leaves.

Charlie and Nia arrive thirty minutes later, and Nia squeals the moment she steps inside her new room. "Mommy, Mommy! This is mine!"

"I know, baby," Charlie says. "It's beautiful."

She turns to me with wide eyes. "Zev, you really didn't have to do this." Then, in a whisper, "We probably won't even be staying here that long."

I refuse to acknowledge the last comment as I am determined to make this their permanent home. The more they like their rooms, the less inclined they will be to leave.

Charlie seems to like hers as well, though she doesn't spend much time in it. I didn't repaint it, but I did change the bedding and lamps, and Sam helped me pick out some trinkets that she said were more "Charlie's vibe."

"I'm sorry to bail on our family date at the last minute," she says with a frown as she wraps her arms around my middle, "but I have to take my car to the mechanic. It's making this crazy sound, and I want to make sure it's not about to break down on me. I should only be gone for an hour. Would you mind watching Nia while I'm gone?"

"Of course not," I tell her. "But why don't I just get you a new car, so this is no longer a source of stress for you?"

She laughs. "Whoa, whoa, whoa. I don't need you to knight-and-shining-armor every little hiccup in my life. You're already helping me with the big stuff, and right now, that's exactly what I need."

I protest for a few more minutes, but eventually I give in.

Once Charlie leaves, I find a spot in the middle of Nia's light gray shag carpet and urge her to open her toy box. She pulls everything out, one at a time, screaming and jumping in place with glee. I expect her to tire herself out by the time the bin is empty, but her energy is a bottomless pit.

As much as she enjoys the new toys, her attention drifts to Otto eventually, which is delightful to watch. She cares for that stuffed dragon more than I cared about anything at her age.

Though I suppose if I had had an object that was soft like a pillow and protected me from danger, I would have been a much happier child. Danger lurked in every corner during my childhood. When it lives beneath the same roof, there is no escaping it. One wrong move, one failed training exercise, there was even a day when, apparently, I breathed too loudly, and it meant hours of blinding pain.

Nia will never have to face such horrors. I will see to that.

"How do dragons fly?" she asks, climbing onto her bed and gliding Otto through the air.

"Their wings are incredibly strong," I tell her, "and can lift them as high as the lowest cloud in the sky, but it's not just that. They also have enough stamina to travel hundreds of miles without needing a break."

"Wow," she says before returning to focus on Otto's route around the edge of her bed. Then she flops onto her back, letting her head hang over the edge as she lifts Otto above her.

I line up her toys in order by size, just to give myself something to do. It's the kind of soothing, meaningless task that brings order into a world that often feels too chaotic for me.

"Are you my dad?" she asks.

My hands still over the bouquet of Lego flowers. Has my heart leaped into my throat? Because it doesn't feel like it's where it should be, and suddenly I feel incapable of swallowing even my own saliva.

"Um, no," I tell her. Saying yes didn't seem like the right answer, even though I wish it were the case. I'm certain if Charlie were here, she'd reply the same way. "It might seem odd that you and your mother are now living with me. I understand that, and it's all right with me if you feel that way."

Am I doing this correctly? I suddenly realize that the words I choose may have a profound effect on Nia, and the last thing I want is to confuse or traumatize her. "I like your mother very much," I say. "You and your mother. I care deeply about both of you. So, for now, you may think of me as your friend." I reach for the dragon toy, and she doesn't hesitate to hand it over. "Like Otto here, my duty is to keep you and your mom safe."

She may credit her stuffed animal for her continued safety, and that's fine by me. Let her think it's Otto. Someday, I hope to show her not only that I am a dragon, but that she has a small army in me and my brothers, all willing to die for her. If she wanted to, this small child could point to a city on the map and order us to burn it to the ground. If it meant keeping her safe, we would do it.

"'Kay," is all she says before hopping down off the bed. "I can do a cartwheel. Wanna see?"

I need to remember how quickly children move from one subject to the next. It's freeing to be in the presence of such a curious and unencumbered mind. "I would love to see."

Gathering the toys in my arms, I drop them into the toy box to make room on the floor, then I climb onto the edge of her bed as she demands so I'm out of her way.

She does a cartwheel. Then another, and another. After five, all perfect form—so I tell her, though I don't actually know what a perfect cartwheel looks like—she grows tired and decides to do a somersault across the furry rug. When her upper body surges forward, her braided pigtail gets caught on the knob of her nightstand, breaking the elastic that's closest to her scalp.

Her hand flies to her hair where the elastic was once whole, and she begins to cry. The sound guts me, and only intensifies as the seconds pass. I have no idea what to do, but I know I don't want to call Charlie. Not because I'm afraid of her reaction, but because I want to show her I can care for Nia myself. I vowed to protect her from all the evils of this world, but I have no experience with styling a child's hair. What if I do it wrong? What if I try to fix it and accidentally pull on her hair, causing her pain?

I'm petrified.

CHAPTER 13

CHARLIE

"*N*ine hundred dollars?" I ask the mechanic. "You're serious? I know it's an older car, but I've kept it in good shape. How can it cost that much?"

"It's a blown head gasket, ma'am. With the parts and labor, anywhere else, you're looking at about fifteen hundred. I'm giving you a deal."

Why is it so damn expensive just to exist? I don't throw around money like some high roller, but it seems like every time I finally catch up on bills or I bring my credit card balances down to a manageable amount, something happens that completely obliterates that progress.

Zev offered to buy me a new car, but I don't want that. I'm not comfortable with handouts. It's bad enough that I need him to remain married to me so I can keep Nia away from Evan. I can't have him buying me a new car too. Not that I'd complain. A new car that doesn't scream at me while I'm driving it sure sounds nice, but it's too much.

"I'm sorry, but I can't commit to that right now," I tell the man. "I'll have to move some money around first."

He nods. "Understood. We offer payment plans, just so you know. No interest for the first twelve months."

"Okay, I'll think about it."

I pull out of the parking lot, and my car starts to bounce as I reach the first red light. A second later, my phone rings. I don't recognize the number. It's sitting on top of my purse in the passenger seat, and I put it on speaker to answer. "Hello?"

"Hey, it's Caitlyn. I hope you don't mind, but I got your number from your marriage license."

That seems like a complete violation of privacy, but she's probably calling with information I need, so I let it slide. "No worries. What's up?"

"I saw in the system that Evan filed for custody. You should be served in the next few days."

"Fuck," I groan, resting my head against the steering wheel. A loud honk sounds from behind me, and when I look up, I see the light has changed to green. "Well, I guess that was inevitable."

"I know this isn't what you wanted, but you haven't lost yet. There are four judges that preside over custody hearings, and I can tell you that with all of them, you need to play it cool."

"What do you mean?"

"He's a narcissist, right?"

"The biggest."

"My ex-husband is a narcissist too. The key to beating them is don't engage. He's going to do everything he can to get you to react. He knows which buttons to push to upset you, and he will push them. All of them. Once you look emotional in court, whichever judge you get will see you as unstable, and Evan will get his way."

"Do they really expect me to be a robot up there when the safety of my child is at stake?"

Caitlyn grunts. "It's bullshit, I know, but once you're playing defense against this guy, you've lost. Don't let him pull you into an outburst. These men don't know how to deal with emotions unless it's their own pent-up, unprocessed rage exploding out of them through the barrel of a gun. Then, somehow, it's perfectly normal."

"What am I supposed to do if he makes me look like a bad mom?"

"You bring it back to the facts," she says, her voice hardening. "The facts are what matter, and it's what the judge wants. You bring pictures of Zev's house: the interior. Show them the room Nia is staying in. Make sure he brings his bank statements. Get character witnesses from her teachers, your dad, and the girls. His brothers too. Whenever Evan starts pulling you toward an argument, you resist the urge to bash his face in and you show the judge that Nia already has everything she needs, and that sharing custody with him will disrupt the comfortable life you've built for her."

It makes sense, even though I hate how easy it is for this whole thing to fall apart. "What about the abuse? Should I even bother talking about that? Establishing a pattern of behavior?"

"Like what?" she asks. "Can you give me some specifics?"

I try to keep my breathing steady as the memories come flooding back. Running away helped me forget. It was easy to focus on getting settled in a new place where there weren't constant reminders of Evan and how he treated me. But now he's here, and even though this isn't where he hurt me, his very presence brings it all back.

"One time, he thought I was having an affair with the chief of staff of our opponent," I explain. "I met this guy—this sixty-four-year-old man, mind you—once over lunch to discuss partnering on a child safety initiative, and Evan called me a whore and broke my glasses in half. When I threatened to call the cops, he grabbed me by the throat, took my phone and threw it into the street."

"Christ," Caitlyn mutters in disgust.

"Then there was the Christmas ball," I begin, my shoulders shaking as the words come out in a rush. "I wore this beautiful, off-the-shoulder tulle A-line gown in gold. It was Mac Duggal, and I saved for months so I could afford it. Anyway, I got my hair and makeup done for the event. I felt like a goddess...

"But when Evan picked me up, he was furious at how much skin I was showing. It wasn't even that much, given that it was a floor-length gown. I was rocking some cleavage, sure, but other than that, it was just my shoulders and back."

"You don't have to justify it to me, Charlie," Caitlyn says. I didn't even realize that's what I was doing until she pointed it out. Old habits die hard. "My ex was controlling with my outfits too. If I had a shoulder or even a collarbone showing when we went out, he'd tell me I should pay for my part of the date by spending a few hours on a street corner."

"Your husband said that to you?" I ask, wishing the emotion I felt was shock, but it's more of a combination of disgust and rage. "The man who's supposed to cherish you in sickness and in health?"

"Ha!" she laughs, her tone dripping with sarcasm. "That man cherished me for all of five minutes over the course of our entire marriage. Most of the time, he complained that my cooking wasn't good enough, or that the house was too dirty, even though we both worked full-time jobs. I was still expected to do the invisible labor and never bother him about it."

I let out a weary groan. My bones are tired. I'm so sick of this being the norm. "Men."

She chuckles in agreement. "Whatever your gown looked like, I'm sure it was appropriate for the occasion."

"It was," I tell her. "I got so many compliments on it, which only made Evan angrier. We left after about an hour, and he screamed at me the whole way home. He was driving, and there were so many moments where he wasn't paying attention and started to drift into oncoming traffic. I was sure we were going to die that night, and I remember hoping we would, if only to avoid what would happen once we were home. I knew it would only get worse from there." My eyes sting with tears as I relive it. "We got back to my place, and before we were even out of the car, he yanked on the skirt of my dress and tore it at the seam. I don't remember exactly what he was saying, something about how I might as well show off my pussy too since I was so desperate for male attention."

Caitlyn gasps. "Fucking pig."

"We got inside," I continue through short, quick breaths, "and I was crying because my dress was ruined. I was apologizing to Evan, trying to get him to calm down. It didn't work, and..." I trail off. The memory becomes too real. "And he—"

"Hey," Caitlyn interrupts. "You don't have to say anymore. It's okay. My mind can fill in the blanks."

I focus on my breath; thankful Caitlyn stopped me from continuing. Remembering that night is painful enough, and I wish I didn't even have that. Why couldn't my brain shut down like it does for some people during moments of extreme trauma? Locking the agony of that night in a box deep inside my mind that I'd never have to open.

"Did you report it to the police at the time or take pictures of your bruises?" she asks.

I sigh, my entire body sagging with disappointment. "No. Neither." There was no way I was involving the police, not when it could so easily backfire on me. And I should've taken pictures, but I wanted to forget it ever happened.

"Very reasonable."

"So...should I bring it up?"

She sighs. "Don't bother. If it comes down to a he-said-she-said, you'll lose."

My car continues to shake and lets out a low, grinding wail as I pull into Zev's massive driveway. "Okay, I'm at Zev's, so I have to go, but thank you for the heads up, and for walking me through this. You didn't have to do that, and I really appreciate it."

I never thought people could change. Not really. But the woman Sam and Vanessa have described compared to the woman I'm talking to now, it's like night and day. I'm not naïve enough to think that people who are nice to one person are nice to everyone, but Caitlyn doesn't seem like the type to be anyone's lackey. I can tell that she's tired of being pushed around and doesn't want to see others endure the same treatment. That's a sign of good character, in my opinion.

"Good luck," she says before disconnecting the call.

I knock on the door before realizing that I'll soon live here and my daughter is inside, so I barge right in. "Hello, fam-uh," I start to say before catching myself. It's too soon for that. "Anyone home?"

There's noise coming from Nia's room, so I follow it.

"In here," Nia calls out when I reach the door. She's sucking on a juice box and sitting on her desk chair as she watches *Moana* on an iPad. With his phone resting sideways on his knee, Zev sits right behind her, perched on the edge of her bed. A comb rests between his teeth, and a bottle of hair oil is pinned between his thighs. His hands are wrapped around her hair as he braids one side, and he looks down at the video on his phone every few seconds. "Hi, Mommy," she says with a wave.

It's then that Zev notices my presence. Without letting go of her hair, Zev spits out the comb and smiles. "Ah, you're back. Nia's elastic broke, so I'm repairing this pigtail. I should be done soon."

Words fail me. My heart melts inside my chest, and my knees grow weak. The scene in front of me is too exquisite to mar with a verbal reaction. I'd rather not disturb the calm energy emanating from my daughter as this white man styles her hair, or the magnificent specimen taking the time to learn how to handle natural hair with a gentle touch and the right tools.

"You had hair oil?" I ask as I sit next to him on the bed.

"No," he says, carefully threading the braid together. "When I tried using one of my elastics, Nia said it wasn't the right kind, so I looked up a few videos on YouTube and asked Sam to run out and grab what I needed."

"Ooh, this is the fancy kind too," I marvel, giving it a whiff. "You see this, Nia? Auntie Sam got you the good stuff."

"Mmm-hmm," she says, her attention still entirely on the movie.

I lean my head on Zev's shoulder as he finishes the braid and adds an elastic to the bottom. "I can't believe you did this."

He pulls back to look down at me. His brow furrows, and I wonder if this is what he'll look like in ten years; those lines deepening into his forehead and around his mouth. He'll still be just as gorgeous, if not more so. "Did what? Fix her hair?"

I inspect the pigtail. "It looks great."

"It won't take me as long next time."

Next time. I love the sound of that.

"How is your car?" he asks. "Did they fix it?"

"Ugh, no. The estimate they gave me was way too high." I start calculating how much credit I have available across my four credit cards and wonder if they'll let me split it evenly. "It's okay. I'll get it fixed. It's just too much right now."

"Your car is here?" he asks, abruptly getting to his feet.

"Yeah," I reply, slightly annoyed that my pillow is now gone. "Why?"

I follow him as he goes outside and stands at my driver's side door. He places his hands on his hips and stares at it. "May I have the keys?"

"Sure." I pull them from my pocket and toss them over. What does he think is going to happen? That it'll magically stop making that horrible noise once he's behind the wheel?

He gets in and starts the car. Then, almost as quickly, he turns the car off and climbs out. "What did they tell you was wrong with it?"

"A blown head gasket."

A smirk tugs at the corners of his lips. "Clever," he says to himself. "Why don't you get Nia, and we'll go back to the mechanic? I'd like to have a word with him."

"Why? What's the point?"

"Trust me."

We take Nia's booster seat from my car and put it in the back of his black Cadillac Escalade, and he follows me to the repair shop. When we arrive, Zev parks his car next to mine and rolls the back windows down as I stand next to my door. He asks me to point out which employee I spoke to. The man walking out of the shop is the same guy from earlier, and when he approaches, I swear I can hear Zev grinding his teeth.

"Hello, sir," Zev begins. "I'm wondering why you lied to this stunning woman to my right about what's wrong with her car. Can you explain that to me?"

"Uh, I'm sorry," the man stammers. "I'm not sure what you're talking about."

"Well, you see, this car needs new spark plugs, yet you told her the issue is a blown head gasket. Now, I'm assuming you chose the head gasket because the signs of necessary repair are similar between the two, yet one service costs upward of three hundred dollars, and the other costs close to a thousand."

Holy shit. How is he doing this?

The man looks between me and Zev, his eyes wide with dread. He's been caught, and he has no idea what to do about it.

"I admit," Zev continues, "it's a clever tactic. You probably get away with it ninety-nine percent of the time." My new husband crosses his arms, the veins in his forearms bulging in the most delicious way. "But today is not your day. Today, you are going to fix what actually needs fixing, and you're going to do it for free because I don't appreciate being lied to or seeing those I care about being lied to. Do you understand me?"

I've never seen this side of Zev before. Here I thought boyish virgin Zev was hot. Bossy, protective Zev is a ball of fucking fire.

"Here's what will happen if you don't," he continues, stepping closer to the terrified mechanic. "I will come back here, buy up the land around your unscrupulous little shop, and surround you with honest mechanics who won't rip off hardworking people until you lose everything and have to close your doors. You'll leave here with only the clothes on your back and your tail between your legs. Oh, and the legacy of utter failure."

"Mommy, what's Zev doing?" Nia asks from the back seat.

"It's okay, baby. He's taking care of something for me," I tell her, completely distracted by the thickness of Zev's neck and the way he's cracking his knuckles while he threatens the mechanic. This man is dangerous in all the right ways. I fan myself with my hand as I enjoy the show.

"Y-yes, sir."

"My name is Zev Monroe," he growls through gritted teeth. "And that is my wife, Charlie. Do not take advantage of her again. Do you hear me?"

His wife. His *wife*. Jesus Christ. I'm tempted to lie down on the pavement with my legs spread in a wide V after that exchange.

How did I ever pity this man? He might not say the right thing all the time or come off as naturally charismatic, but there's no one else I'd want on my side in a crisis. That much is clear.

I can't stop staring at Zev on the drive home. He turns and asks if

I'm okay a few times, but when I assure him that I'm just fine, he blushes as if he can feel my need for him.

When we get back to his place, he puts *Moana* on the TV in the living room, and Nia falls asleep between us halfway through. "You should stay the night," Zev says quietly. "If you want, I mean. I need help figuring out what else I need to buy for you two."

"You don't have to buy a single thing," I remind him. "You've already spent too much on us as it is."

"I want you to be comfortable here."

"We are." I look down at Nia, who's snoring away as drool drips from her mouth onto Zev's T-shirt. "She certainly is."

Zev chuckles warmly as he tucks the fuzzy blanket around Nia's shoulders, and my heart squeezes with the wish that he was her biological father. He seems like he'd be a fantastic dad.

"In fact," I say, carefully removing myself from under Nia's blanket, "I have a few ideas on how to make me more comfortable, if you'll just come with me real quick."

He looks confused at first, but gently lowers Nia's head onto the couch as he gets to his feet and follows me toward his room. I grab his hand and pull him inside, leaving the door cracked enough that I can hear Nia if she calls for me.

"Do you need a hypoallergenic comforter?" Zev asks once we're alone. "Because I wondered about that—"

"Shut up and kiss me." I reach up, twisting my fingers in his hair and pulling his face down until I feel his breath fan across my cheek. His lips are frozen when they meet mine, but then they become hot and demanding. He takes control of the kiss, nibbling and sucking on my bottom lip in a way that curls my toes.

I moan into his mouth, and he pulls me against him, my body pressed against the hard lines of his stomach. His hips grind against me as nails dig into his scalp, both of us seeking friction, any and all that we can find. He opens for me, and I twirl my tongue around his, exploring the depths of his mouth. I suck in a breath when he nips at the tip of my tongue, my nerves jolting me awake in a way my body has never been.

"Charlie," he growls, his soft lips leaving a wet trail across the line of my jaw and down my neck. His hands move south until they're gripping the globes of my ass. "So sweet, my angel."

It feels good, amazing, but it's not enough. I need more. I need him everywhere. Turning in his arms, I press my back against the wall that is his chest and place his hands right where I want them—one on my breast, and the other down the waist of my leggings. "Yes," I whimper, his broad fingers squeezing my nipple through my thin T-shirt and bralette almost to the point of pain. "More."

I arch into his touch as he slips his hand beneath my panties, his hand pressing against my aching clit. He groans as he bites into my shoulder, and I feel his hard length thrusting against the cleft of my ass. I want nothing more than to strip him down and fuck him right here on the floor of his bedroom, but it's too risky. Nia could hear us, or god forbid, walk in on us.

Plus, I'm not sure Zev is ready for that. I won't push that boundary until I know he's comfortable, and right now, this seems like as far as he's willing to go. Fine by me, because the moment his finger glides through my slick folds, my knees buckle. The only reason I'm not on the ground is because he's holding me up. I'm wrapped tightly in his embrace as he adds another finger, my walls clenching around him as I watch his thick wrist flick back and forth.

"Feels good?" he asks, his breath hot against my neck.

"Mmm," I moan, gripping his ink-covered forearm like it's a lifeline. "So good."

Wet sounds fill the air, and it only brings me closer to the edge. "Faster," I beg, desperate to come quickly before Nia wakes up. "Please."

He obeys, and my hips start pumping wildly onto his hand. A pool of warmth spreads at my lower back as Zev grunts into my hair, but it doesn't slow him down.

"Come for me," he whispers, sinking his teeth into the shell of my ear. My body seizes with the force of my release, my vision blurring as Zev strokes my stomach and mutters words I can't make out against my back.

We start to come down, our chests heaving as he holds me up. My legs feel like noodles as I try to stand on my own. He turns me in his arms, cradling my face in his hands, and presses a kiss to my forehead. That kiss feels more intimate than the entirety of what we just did, and I worry I won't be able to walk out of this room without his arms around me. I worry I won't be able to exist from this day forward without the comfort I feel in the safety of his embrace.

"Oh my god," I mutter, still trying to catch my breath.

"Yeah?" he asks, that wolfish grin returning. That's the smirk of a man who knows how to please his woman. It looks good on him.

"Yeah," I reply, leaning up on my tiptoes to nip at his chin.

"Mommy?" Nia cries out, her voice rough with sleep.

"Coming, baby."

Zev drops his hand in front of his pants with a shy smile. "I'll, uh, be right out. I just need to change."

Good. I'm glad I'm not the only one who enjoyed that.

CHAPTER 14

ZEV

*I*t's getting increasingly difficult to resist having sex with Charlie. I want to. *God do I want to,* but doing so will solidify our bond as mates for eternity. She will be mine in every sense of the word, and she still doesn't know what I am. Well, I don't think she knows. Technically, I told her, but she likely doesn't remember. And I'm not sure what to do about that.

Even now as I feast upon her pussy in the early morning hours, it takes all my strength to not climb up her voluptuous body and sink my cock into her wet heat.

Her small hands grip my hair as she presses my face against her slick folds, demanding everything I have to give. "Fuck, Zev! Yes!"

In the nights that have followed our little encounter in my bedroom, she has tucked Nia into bed, then snuck into my room where we spend hours exploring each other's bodies with our mouths and hands. We've learned to remain quiet so as not to alert Nia to our activities. Yet my ravenous mate seems to have forgotten the rules.

"Shh, my sweet," I whisper, playfully nipping at her inner thigh. "You can't be so loud."

She presses a pillow against her face as I resume my ministrations. Running my tongue along her seam, I pause at the swollen bud at the top, flicking the tip of my tongue across it at a rapid pace. Her taste is extraordinary, and part of me wonders if I could survive on her sweet nectar alone. I bet I could.

Her body trembles as I insert a finger into her core, and it appears she's already close to the edge. Eager to push her off, I suck on her clit, changing the pressure of my lips based on her body's reactions. She screams into the pillow as her thighs squeeze the sides of my head, but I don't stop. I don't even slow my pace. My tongue circles and swipes, circles and swipes her clit, just as her own fingers did in my car that night, until she's boneless and spent atop my rumpled sheets.

"Feel better, wife?" I ask as I climb up her soft, supple body and pull her into my arms.

"Definitely," she says, her voice raspy from screaming. "You made me forget about the hearing for a whole thirty minutes. Thank you for that."

She was served with papers at her dad's house yesterday and has been a wreck ever since. She knew it was coming thanks to Caitlyn's call, but it didn't make it easier to face when it finally happened.

Yesterday was also when she chose to tell her father that we got married. I wish I had been there to explain how much I love his daughter and will spend the rest of my days making her smile, but Charlie insisted it was better coming from her, and in private. When she got home, she told me he didn't seem mad, just confused. But he needed to know in order to provide a character statement for the hearing, and he told her that as long as she was happy, he was happy for her.

I told her I'd no longer be attending her guitar class. It seems silly, at this point, to continue the ruse, though I do have a plan for the final test. I'm certain I'll pass, and I'm hoping she truly enjoys what I've prepared for her.

Her Honda Civic was repaired at no charge, and while I'm glad it's no longer a source of stress, it seems when one problem gets resolved, another arises. On Monday of this week, she was told by the elementary school principal that budget cuts have forced them to reduce her twice-weekly music classes down to a monthly music practice with all the kids from grades three through five.

I assured her that she doesn't have to teach the kids at all, or the adults, or even work at the library, if she chooses not to. I have enough money for us to live comfortably for several centuries and never work again, but she refused and said financial independence is important to her, and she likes the jobs she has.

It baffles me that she's so reluctant to rely on me, her husband, after what we've been through. Isn't this the point of being married? You no longer have to face the world alone. You tackle each obstacle as a formidable team. No matter how much time we spend together, she acts like she's still facing her problems alone. I'd give anything to ease the pain she carries.

"Do we have to get up?" Charlie whines as the sun peeks through the thick velvet curtains in my room. "I wanna stay here all day."

I kiss along her collarbone, then down her right arm. "We don't have to pick up Nia until lunch, right?"

She yawns. "Yeah, Dad and Joyce wanted to take her out to breakfast after their sleepover."

"When is Joyce moving in?"

"Uh, I think…" Charlie begins, but her words stop as the walls begin to shake, the window rattling so hard, it sounds as if it's moments away from shattering. "What the hell?"

I pull her down to the floor on top of me, next to the bed, unsure of what to do. "Stay here," I tell her, wrapping the sheet around my waist as I crawl toward the window. Branches snap outside, and the wind whips violently against the side of the house.

"Is it a tornado?" Charlie asks, huddling beneath the comforter. "I need to get to Nia."

Peering out the window at our front yard, I watch in horror as two funnel clouds drop down next to each other. I would think they were tornadoes, if not for the different colors. One has a dark gray, almost black shade, and the other is bright red.

"No, not tornadoes," I tell Charlie, my stomach tightening into a painful knot. "Something much worse."

The clouds spread horizontally, revealing two massive dragons, one black and one red. Then, a flicker of light appears, blocking them from view, and what remains are a pair of large men as tall as my brothers and me, if not taller, dressed very differently from each other.

The one on the left has pitch-black hair, short on the sides, but longer on top and styled neatly. He wears a crisp white button-up shirt that's entirely too tight. I can see every ab on his stomach through that shirt. His pants are slightly looser, and he wears brown leather loafers with no socks.

The man next to him has long, wavy red hair that hangs wildly around his broad shoulders. He wears a green cable-knit sweater with a hole in the sleeve and along the bottom hem. His pants are loose dark jeans tucked into tall lace-up boots.

I think I know who they are, but I desperately hope I'm wrong. Crawling over to my nightstand, I grab my phone and call Mylo.

He answers after one ring. "What the fuck was that?"

"You need to get over here right now," I tell him before hanging up.

Charlie crawls over to the window and gasps. "Who are they?"

I pull her down before they can see us.

Then I hear a low, booming voice shout, "I am here for Mylo," sending every bird and woodland creature fleeing the scene as fast as their bodies and wings will take them.

Charlie and I throw our clothes on and stumble outside. I attempt to shield her from this, but when I suggest she stay inside where it's safe, she replies, "Absolutely fucking not."

It seems my time is up. There is no turning back after this.

Kyan stomps out behind us, a murderous look on his face.

"Hello," I greet the large strangers. "I am Zev. This is my wife, Charlie. And you are?"

"Ah, you are mated!" the dark-haired one says, clapping his hands together. I can tell by his voice that he's the one who yelled for Mylo. His accent is thick, and it sounds Italian. "How lovely. You know, I have never been one for these formalities the humans hold so dear, but it is nice to see that there are some who find value in such traditions."

"The humans?" Charlie whispers, looking at me like the man in front of us might be unwell, and I wish I could play along.

Mylo and Sam come charging through the woods from the direction of their new house and skid to a stop right next to us.

"Don't...ever...make me...run that fast...again," Sam says through panting breaths. She's doubled over with her hands resting on her knees. "That sucked."

I slap Mylo's arm and push him forward.

"I'm Mylo," he says. "Nice to meet you."

"Ah, this one," the redhead mutters, his accent even thicker, but unlike the other. Scottish, I think.

"Mylo," the dark-haired one says. "I am Dante Moretti, and this is my brother tikano, Ronan MacLeod."

"I'm sorry, your brother what?" Mylo asks.

Sam looks at me. "Zev, should Charlie be here right now?"

Charlie looks between me and Sam, her eyes swirling with worry. "What do you mean?"

"Tikano is our kind," Dante explains, ignoring Sam and Charlie. "We hail from Planet Nocturna Tora, and the three of us were elated to feel your presence in my country. We were disappointed though when you left without paying us a visit."

Kyan laughs. "Wait, the three of you? I think your math is wrong."

"Planet what now?" Charlie asks, picking up on the exact words I was so hoping she would miss.

Dante smiles. "Ah, yes, well our third brother tikano was occupied in his beloved Iceland and could not step away to come see you." I'm not sure how to describe Dante other than bouncy. He's mostly on the balls of his feet, with his hands moving as quickly as the words fall from his lips. It is very strange.

While the other male, Ronan, stands perfectly still, glowering at us.

"Oh, so you're the ones Mylo felt while we were in Siena," Sam says in a tone far too upbeat than is appropriate for what's unfolding before us. Her stance changes from guarded and stiff to open and welcoming. She is not helping. "We were so worried that day, you know? It was our honeymoon, and Mylo couldn't tell if you were good or evil, so we just fucking bolted out of there."

Mylo nods, laughing nervously, I think. I can't tell.

Dante closes the distance between him and Sam. "Oh no, no, no, *signora*, we come in peace, as the aliens on your films would say," he says with a chuckle. "We are like you. Cousins, if you will."

Charlie holds up her hands. "I'm sorry...aliens?"

"You know, this might not be the best time for this gathering," I say, emotions warring within me and making my hands shake. "Perhaps we can reschedule."

Dante nods. "We have been rude, dropping by like this without an invitation." He gives Sam a kiss on each cheek, then throws an arm over Mylo's shoulder. "We have much to discuss, cousin. Give me your phone, and I will put in my number."

Mylo obeys, not as reluctant as I'd expect him to be, considering two dragon shifters from another planet showed up at our door and one of them kissed his mate.

"I'd like that," Mylo says as Dante hands his phone back. Mylo calls the number, and when Dante's phone rings, his smile stretches from ear to ear. "*Fantastico.* Now I have yours, and we shall be in touch, yes?" Dante turns to walk toward the woods but stops in his tracks. "We are staying in a house on, uh," he turns to Ronan, "what is it called?"

"Lake Winnipesaukee," Ronan mutters.

"Ah, yes. Beautiful views," Dante says proudly. "Just beautiful."

They disappear into the woods a few minutes later, and the silence hangs heavy above us. I feel Charlie's eyes boring a hole into my head. "Uh, what the fuck, Zev?"

CHAPTER 15

CHARLIE

*M*ylo ushers us inside and calls Axil. He and Vanessa show up a few minutes later, along with Luka and Harper. Earlier this week, I met Harper, her vet tech, Ryan, and Luka and Harper's two sons. I'm glad Ryan and the two boys aren't here to witness the batshit conversation I'm about to have, but I'm not so glad we have such a huge audience.

"I think we need to talk privately, don't you?" I say to Zev, gesturing for him to follow me to his room.

"Actually," Sam pipes in, "it'll be easier for you to have the rest of us here. I promise."

Hard disagree. "Why is that?"

Vanessa wipes the sleep from her eyes and lets out a loud yawn. "Because Sam and I have both been exactly where you are and leaving it up to the guys to explain has not gone well."

"And by *explain*, you mean the whole alien thing? Or the weird men who just appeared in your front yard out of nowhere after the house almost fell down? Or the fact that they walked into the woods back to their vacation rental on Lake Winnipesaukee, which is an hour away?"

"All of it," Sam replies. "They're all part of the same thread."

The more they speak, the less it makes sense, and I'm starting to get a cluster headache behind my right eye. "Can someone start from the beginning? Am I dreaming? Let's start there."

Mylo coughs. "Zev, you're up."

Zev reaches for me, but I pull away. I can't let him touch me again until I understand what the fuck I just saw. "Charlie, you are not dreaming."

When he doesn't continue, I throw up my hands. "Okay, and?"

He lets out a slow, shaky breath. "The men who were in our yard are not human. They are aliens...from planet, um," he looks at Mylo. "What was it?"

"Nocturna Tora."

"Right, Nocturna Tora." Zev swallows. "I don't know where that planet is, but they said they are tikano, which is a species of what you would call dragon shifters."

"Dragon shifters?" I ask. "As in they go from men to dragons? Flying dragons with wings and scales and fiery breath and all that?"

"Yes," Zev nods, looking encouraged that I'm following along. Encouraged is not the emotion I would choose. He should be nervous. Very fucking nervous. "We, my brothers and I, are another species of dragon shifter called draxilios, and we hail from planet Sufoi."

I can't believe I'm about to ask the following question. "You're telling me you're not human?"

"Correct."

Sam gets to her feet and stands at Charlie's side. "I know it sounds bananas, but he's telling the truth. None of the men in this room are human, and the women in this room found out just like you did."

"Well, I didn't," Harper says, leaning on the cushioned handle of her hand-carved wooden cane. "I found out while we were having sex. Luka's eyes turned red and holy hell, I have never been so scared. I thought he was dying."

"Wait, your eyes turn red?" I ask, my mind starting to spin.

"See, a draxilio's eyes turn red when he finds his mate," Zev explains. "It's the moment the two parts of him become aligned in the knowledge that the one they're meant to spend their life with is standing before them. It's a signal, if you will."

My gaze drifts to Mylo and Axil. "And that happened to you too?"

They nod in unison.

"Yours haven't turned yet," I say to Zev. "What does that mean?"

"They have!" he says excitedly. "That's why I skipped those two classes. My eyes turned after Nia hugged me in the library." He reaches for my hands, and this time, I don't move away. "I knew you were my mate from the very beginning, my draxilio did as well, but my eyes didn't turn until I met Nia, which tells me that her approval was needed in order for the signal to work."

I don't know how long I stand there trying to process what he said, but it feels like a long time. It feels real, but also ridiculous. Aliens exist? And I'm married to one? No. That can't be true. That's nonsense.

I'd assume it was total bullshit if it weren't for Sam, Vanessa, and Harper. The glances they exchange while this is going on tells me that this is real, and the shocking moment of discovery has happened to each of them. I don't know them very well, but it really doesn't seem like they're lying. It doesn't seem like Zev is lying either.

There's so much I still need to know, but the biggest question I have can't wait any longer. "Why didn't you tell me?"

He scrubs a rough hand down his face. "You see, that's also a bit complicated, because in order for the redness of our eyes to fade, our mate needs to verbally accept what we are. Both parts of us: man and beast. And as you can see, my eyes are not red."

I'm not following. "What does that mean?"

"My eyes were red when I went to Pollo Palace that day. I was wearing contacts to cover them and sunglasses in case the contacts stopped working. When I woke up the next morning, we were married, and my eyes were no longer red. I don't know how to explain it, and I have no memory of it, but I must've told you at some point that night, and you accepted it. You accepted…me."

In spite of everything Zev has just told me, I can't help but crumble a little at the sight of him so afraid. His eyes are wide and rimmed with unshed tears, and he shifts nervously between his feet as he waits for my reaction. He's like an open chest cavity with his beating heart bared for all to see.

"I," I begin, not knowing what I'm about to say, "I can't be here right now." My feet take me toward the door, and I grab my purse off the hook on the wall. "I need to go."

Zev races over and blocks my path. "Wait. Please."

The others start to back away, as if to give us privacy.

I shove my feet into my fur-lined crocs and wait for him to continue.

"Let me ask you something. Say I did tell you that day. Say I told you when you came here and admitted that you were the one who pushed us to get married. You needed me at that moment, Charlie. You still need me now. If I had told you that day, would you have run?"

I don't know the answer to that, but I'm inclined to say yes. What person wouldn't? "Probably," I say with a sigh.

"If you had run, packed up your stuff and Nia and left town, you would still be struggling. Evan would still be looking for you. Your future would remain uncertain, and the stress you carry would be compounded by another move. Another start in a new place where you don't know anyone."

"And?" I fail to see how this is supposed to make me want to stay.

"For as long as you'll let me, I want to take away your stress and replace it with comfort. That's all I've ever wanted to do. I want you and Nia to be safe. You deserve a comfortable life. Your daughter deserves the same. You don't have to do this alone anymore, Charlie," his voice breaks on my name. "We are not meant to be mates, just you and me. We are meant to be a *family*. The three of us. I-I love you, Charlie. More than anything."

Maybe he's right. I would've run again, and I'd always be looking over my shoulder. This is the first time in five years that I've planted my feet in the dirt and chosen to fight back. It wasn't easy, but I feel stronger. I wouldn't have attempted that without Zev. He gave me the support I needed to do that. I wanted to find my village, and I found it in him. He's an entire village in just one body. He's become my closest ally, my teammate, and the love of my life.

I...wait. What? I...*love* him?

I do. I love him.

The word should feel wrong, given what just happened, but it doesn't. It feels right, like a warm embrace in the middle of a hurricane.

I might love him, but am I ready to accept the reality he just dropped at my feet? That, I don't know. What I do know is that I need coffee.

"I'm going for a drive," I tell him. "Let me process this, and I'll be back."

Part of me expects him to follow. To chase me down the driveway and beg me to never leave his side. If not him, then Sam or Vanessa. He doesn't though, and the others don't either. I asked for space, and he gave it to me. The question is, how long do I want to keep it?

I end up at Common Grounds, and Caitlyn happily meets me there. I'm not sure why I feel compelled to talk to her right now, but when I hit my first red light after leaving Zev's, I pulled out my phone and instinctively texted her. She's been so deeply woven into this strange journey Zev and I have been on that it felt right to seek her advice on this, even if I can't give her the truth about what he is.

It's moments like this that make me hate how little diversity there is in Sudbury. Just having one other Black woman I could call would be a like balm for my soul. One friend who would understand what it's like to exist inside this skin and who I could be completely myself around. It's a different kind of sisterhood. Caitlyn is nice, and the other women are too, but it's not the same.

"I hope married life is better than the last time I saw you," she says in greeting.

"It's...had its ups and downs," I mutter as we get in line. "I'd like your thoughts on that, actually."

"My thoughts?" she asks with arched eyebrows. "I'm the opposite of a love guru. You should probably talk to Vanessa or Sam if you want tips on how to maintain a blissful union."

As much as I adore those two, Vanessa and Sam are biased. Not only do they have their own alien-dragon mates to keep hidden from the world, but those mates are also Zev's brothers. They want me to have my happily ever after with their brother-in-law, and I doubt they'll do anything to dissuade me from that path.

Caitlyn knows more about my particular brand of pain, and she understands the kind of evil I'm up against, having been married to a narcissist herself.

Once our drinks are ready, I find a secluded picnic table outside, shielded by beautiful trees with falling auburn leaves.

"So, what's going on?" Caitlyn asks.

I invited her here to talk, and now I have no idea how to begin. "I'm struggling, I guess, with the idea of really committing to Zev," I finally say. "I, uh, I'm not sure if I'm ready for this. Something so serious."

"Seems a little late for that," she says with a chuckle. When she notices the absence of my sense of humor, she clears her throat, and her expression softens. "After things ended with Evan, how many guys did you date monogamously?"

"None," I reply instantly. "I went on a few dates with a few guys, but I never got to the *let's be exclusive* stage."

"How come?"

I can't help but laugh. "Isn't it obvious? Trusting someone again seemed impossible. Borderline stupid even. Plus, I was busy enough with Nia that it didn't feel like there was a void in my life that needed to be filled."

Caitlyn considers this. "Okay, so your relationship with Evan is the most recent template you have for what love looks and feels like."

My stomach lurches at that statement. "Fuck, I guess. I mean, obviously I know how messy it was, and the abuse I endured wasn't my fault…"

Caitlyn finishes my thought. "But everything inside you is clenching up at the possibility of you going down that same road. Your body remembers the trauma and refuses to let it happen again." She takes a sip of her hot vanilla latte and nods sympathetically. "I get it.

Why do you think I've become such a massive slut lately? Casual sex is easy, and it's fucking fun. Relationships though? Trusting another person with all my vulnerabilities? That shit is scary. Like, murderous-clown-in-the-sewer scary."

She's right. I know me and Zev are already married, and I can't deny that I've fallen in love with him, but actually settling into a life with him as my partner is such a giant, terrifying unknown, and Evan hurt me so deeply, that maybe I'm incapable of trusting another person that much. Maybe I'm too broken to heal.

"Zev seems different," Caitlyn points out. "That entire family does. Not just in a physical sense either. They're weird, in a way, but they're not your average men. I haven't spent much time around them, but Axil and Mylo seem to dote on Vanessa and Sam, you know? It's like theirs is an emotional generosity that most guys are incapable of. And Zev's been like that with you too, right?"

I nod.

He has. Zev has been generous with his home, his money, his patience, and his heart. I suppose I'm not used to that.

"Girl, do you have any idea how rare that is?" she asks, slapping her hand on the table. "A man who is truly open about how he feels and doesn't waver on it?" She shakes her head. "What more proof do you need that he's worth the risk?"

Proof. The word plants itself in my mind and echoes long after it leaves Caitlyn's mouth. That's what I need. I need proof that he really is different from the rest of the men in this world, and that he can give me everything he says he wants to. Without proof, it's just words, and words are hollow. He needs to show me that Nia and I will be able to live safely and happily beside him. I won't settle for anything less.

CHAPTER 16

ZEV

I ask everyone to leave after Charlie does. I'm in no mood for company. My mate just walked out the door, and despite what she said, I'm not certain she'll ever return. It was foolish of me to keep this secret for so long. I thought I was helping her, making her life easier by keeping this hidden, but it only made things worse.

My family ignores my request and remains by my side. They stay with me in the living room, saying nothing, just sitting quietly as I wait and hope for Charlie's return.

At one point, Kyan asks, "Should we be worried that she knows the truth about us, and we let her drive away?"

He always chooses the worst times to be himself. "What would you have me do?" I ask. "Lock her in the basement until she agrees to solidify the bond?"

"Very well," he says, rolling his eyes. "What we should be talking about are those sneaky fucking tikanos, Dante and Ronan. Don't call them, Mylo."

"Why not?" Mylo asks. "They don't seem like a threat. If they wanted to attack us for trespassing, they would have."

"It would be good to have an ally outside the U.S.," Luka notes.

"They can alert us to other outsiders who arrive. We need to do more to track that anyway."

Kyan scoffs. "We don't need them for that. In fact, we don't need them for anything."

"Oh, are you saying you have the ability to track aliens entering Earth's atmosphere all by yourself?" Axil asks with a smirk.

"What if I am?" Kyan replies.

Axil, Luka, and Mylo start laughing hysterically. "Is that how you spend your days in your high-rise corporate office?" Luka asks. "Making spreadsheets and hacking into Area 51?"

He storms off, growling as he goes, and flips one of the counter stools in the kitchen as he passes it. One of the legs breaks in three places.

"You're paying for a new one," Mylo shouts.

Kyan shouts back, "You don't even live here anymore!"

A calm settles over the room once Kyan leaves, and another hour passes before Charlie returns. She walks in with a large, iced coffee in hand, kicks off her shoes, hangs her purse on the hook, and strides into the living room.

I scramble to get to my feet as she approaches. "Hi." It was the only thing I felt I could say.

"Here's the deal," she begins. "I'm not sure my brain fully accepts the fact that you're an alien, or a dragon. Or a...dragon/alien. So I'm gonna need some proof."

"Proof?"

"Yes, and I'll need it in two forms. The first: I want to watch you shift into a dragon, and I want to go for a ride. As long as I won't die." She turns to the girls. "I won't die, will I?"

"Nope," they all reply. "We've all done it and it's fucking amazing," Sam says.

"Cool," Charlie says. "The second thing I need, and I need this one now, is proof that you can protect me and my daughter."

"Wouldn't witnessing the shift into his dragon check that box?" Vanessa asks.

"No, because you can't do that out in the open. What if we're in a grocery store and someone pulls out an assault rifle? What if we're driving on the highway and our car flips over?" She holds her arms wide. "This is Earth. You can't openly be a dragon here, or you risk exposing your family. So how are you going to protect us while still pretending to be human?"

I'm not sure how to do that. I want to, more than anything, but that's what has made our lives on Earth so difficult. "What do you have in mind?"

She shrugs. "I don't know. Maybe I'll know it when I see it." Charlie steps around me and sits in the middle of the couch, casually sipping her coffee.

Ah. This is a test. My brilliant mate is testing me. I refuse to let her down.

"Ooh, I know," Vanessa says, "What if I hit Charlie?"

"What?" I ask, shocked by her suggestion.

"No," Axil grunts. "You're pregnant, and you don't know how Zev will react when his mate is threatened."

Vanessa shakes her head. "I wouldn't actually do it. You would stop me before I hit her, showing her that you can protect her."

Kyan strolls back into the room. "That won't work anyway because he knows it's coming. The key is to show her that you can protect her and Nia in an unexpected situation."

"Why are you here?" Mylo asks him.

Kyan flips him off and takes a seat on the arm of the couch.

Out of the corner of my eye, I see Sam sneaking toward the umbrella holder. As she pulls out a wooden walking stick that Axil carved, Mylo races over and yanks it away. "No, no, no. You're not playing this game either."

"Oh come on," Sam whines. "I was just trying to help."

Mylo picks her up and drapes her across his lap in the accent chair.

My brothers continue to offer suggestions that don't make sense. This goes on for several minutes. The constant bickering creates a ringing in my ears, and I'm tempted to scream to make it stop.

A metallic flash catches my eye, and I watch as Kyan grabs a silver laptop off the kitchen counter and hurls it across the room, heading straight for the back of Charlie's head.

Instinctively, I leap over her, clearing the couch entirely as my fingers wrap around the smooth exterior of the computer. Before my feet touch the ground, I summon the electrical current still within the device and throw it back. The laptop unfolds in midair, and the air around us starts to crackle as the laptop closes around Kyan's face like an open book.

He lets out a bellowing cry that's muffled by the sound of tiny bolts of electricity striking him in the face and neck, causing him to stagger backward and collapse onto the kitchen floor. Every light in the house begins to flicker, and it takes a moment before I realize I'm causing it.

Eventually, a hush falls over the room, and the only thing we hear is the soft charring of Kyan's burned skin.

I might've just killed my brother.

CHAPTER 17

CHARLIE

...I think I just witnessed a murder. Committed by my husband. Did I really think this day couldn't get worse? Because it just got worse.

Suddenly, Kyan tosses the laptop off his face and leaps to his feet, howling with laughter. I stand there stunned and terrified by what I just saw. The burns running down his face start to fade before my eyes.

"Sorry, Charlie," Kyan says, wiping the tears from his eyes. His skin is already healed. No burn marks or blisters remain. That took seconds, and he's completely healed. "I assure you, it wasn't personal, but I knew that was the only way he could prove it."

"Fucking asshole," Zev groans at his brother's antics, but walks around the couch and kneels before me. "I'm sorry I didn't tell you before, but I have the ability to communicate with machines. Did I frighten you?" he asks.

Only then do I replay the last few minutes in my head. I didn't see Kyan throw the laptop, and I barely caught Zev jumping over my head—over my fucking head!—to block it. What I did see was the laptop flying back toward Kyan at top speed, the laptop somehow electrocuting Kyan when it hit him in the face, and the lights flickering like a thousand ghosts were summoned. And all of that...Zev did. My husband.

Maybe I should be frightened, but I'm not. The list of things I'm afraid of when I wake up in the morning is endless. Zev isn't on that list. If anything, I've never felt safer. It's difficult to see how much fear consumes you until it's gone. I've spent my entire adult life crippled with fear. But Zev isn't going to let anything happen to me or my daughter, and a man who makes me feel safe is not something I'm willing to let go of.

"I don't know if you can do that in the middle of the grocery store without raising some eyebrows, but I admit, that was impressive."

Zev pulls me into his arms and rocks me back and forth. "I'm sorry. I let you down and I'm sorry."

"It's okay," I tell him, stroking my hand over his hair. "We're okay."

* * *

"Are you sure you want to do this?" Zev asks for the tenth time since we walked into the clearing behind their house.

"Ugh, yes, I'm sure." I run my hand along one of the blue tarps hanging from the trees, blocking the view of his draxilio from any trespassers. "I can't be the only mate in the group who hasn't gotten her dragon ride."

Is this really my life? Am I about to ride my alien-dragon husband across the sky?

Bouncing on my feet, I wait patiently as Zev shakes out his arms and legs, loosening the muscles in his body. He said the shift doesn't hurt, but it might look like it does, and I shouldn't worry. The air crackles around us, the same way it did when he was controlling the lights.

Bones crack, and the ground shakes as the transformation begins. He's right, it does look painful. I wince as I watch his body stretch and break to accommodate his other, much larger form. Soon enough, the space between the tarps is filled with a massive blue dragon.

He's the size of a school bus, maybe two. When he smiles, I curl in on myself because his teeth are like long, sharp swords. I open my eyes when a loud snuffle lifts the ends of my hair and speckles of saliva spray across the backs of my hands.

It's Zev, or the other part of Zev, rather, trying to say hello. Timidly, I pat the end of his snout, and I'm surprised by how beautiful and smooth his scales are. They each have the same wide range of shimmering blue colors, but some scales have teal diamonds, some have navy-blue octagons, and some have baby-blue triangles. I could spend the day studying his scales, and I'm sure I'd discover a small detail on each one that's entirely different from the others.

"Hi, there," I say, trying to mask my nerves. "It's an honor to finally meet you."

The beast leans into my touch, closing his eyes as he presses harder into my hand. How can such a large, dangerous creature be so gentle? I suppose that sums Zev up in a nutshell. He's always been dangerous and capable of spectacular, horrifying things, but he doesn't let me see that side unless he's protecting me from someone else.

My dragon opens his huge claw, and nods toward it, gesturing for me to climb inside. I hadn't considered being curled up inside his claw when I asked for this dragon flight, but it certainly seems like the safest mode of transportation.

Carefully, I climb inside and sit cross-legged in the center. His claws close around me, and I peek through his fingers as he brings me against his chest.

The moment he leaps into the air, I start screaming. I don't remember anything after that. Not the ride, not the view—nothing. At some point, I wake up on the ground inside the tarps with Zev holding me in his arms.

"Charlie," he says, his voice thick with emotion. "I was so worried."

"What happened? Did we fly? Was it awesome?"

He chuckles. "We flew, but I don't think you found it to be awesome. I heard you screaming and immediately turned around. You were unconscious in my hand when we landed."

"Fuuck, really?" I whine. That's disappointing, but I suppose he can't eradicate all my fears. I didn't realize flying or heights were on that list, but you learn something new every day. "I'm sorry."

"Why are you sorry?" he asks, helping me to my feet. "We can try it another time, if you wish, but maybe it isn't for you. That's okay. My draxilio understands."

I'm relieved to hear that. I don't want the beast inside my husband to resent me.

"I don't know if we should tell Nia. Not just yet," I tell him as we walk back to the house.

He nods. "It's a heavy secret to carry for such a young mind. We shouldn't burden her with it."

"Okay, good," I say with a sigh. "I'm glad you agree."

"There's plenty of time," he assures me. Taking my hand, he leads me back to the house.

Everyone has dispersed by now, going back to their own houses and resuming their days. It's just the two of us, it seems. "We've got the house to ourselves," I tell Zev, walking backward toward the kitchen until my ass hits the counter. Then I reach for the nape of his neck and pull his face down until I can press my lips to his.

Desire surges through me as his fingers dig into my lower back, holding me tightly against his hard body. His mouth opens for me, his tongue hot as it slides against mine. He groans, and my entire body quivers at the sound. I feel his hardness through his pants, and it's like an impossibly long steel pole. There's nothing I want more right now than to have him inside me, stretching and filling and using my body for his own pleasure, wringing ecstasy out of me until I pass out. But I need the real him.

I break the kiss, his mouth swollen and his hair a mess, most of it loose from his bun, and say, "Unmask for me."

He obeys my command, his horns ascending from his hairline and those beautiful blue scales taking the place of his pale human skin.

I stroke along his forehead and jaw. "I still can't believe you're real," I whisper, tracing the curve of his horns.

"I'm real, and I'm yours," he tells me, wrapping his hands around my waist and lifting me onto the kitchen island.

A little yelp of surprise falls from my lips when my feet leave the floor, and he presses a gentle but firm finger against my mouth in warning, just in case anyone else is home.

He guides me onto my back and pushes the hem of my shirt up, taking my thin bralette with it, exposing my breasts to the chilly air of the house. He licks his lips as my nipples harden, and then descends upon my chest with an open, hungry mouth.

My back arches and my nails dig into the thick, corded muscles of his arms as he sucks and licks my nipple, his free hand squeezing and massaging the other. When he closes his teeth around the stiff peak of my breast, I cry out, pressing his palm against my lips to help quiet me. "Don't stop," I whimper against his hand.

He pulls his hand from my mouth to trail his fingers down my chest, then stomach. His touch is slow and reverent as he gazes down at my exposed skin with pure adoration in his eyes. I've never felt more beautiful.

Zev's hand slips beneath the waist of my sweatpants, and a growl rumbles deep in his chest the moment he strokes through my curls and traces my slit. His eyes fall closed as he lets out a shuddering breath. "You feel so good, Charlie."

I wrap my legs around him as his lips return to my chest, giving the other breast the same focused attention he gave the first. My body moves on its own, grinding against his hand as he slips a finger inside me. "Yes," I moan.

"What the fuck?" Kyan shouts as he stomps down the stairs.

I let out a string of curses as I rush to cover myself, but Zev uses his upper body to cover me, placing his hands on either side of my head, not letting Kyan see even a speck of my skin.

"Yeah, what the fuck?" Zev shouts back. "Are you watching us, you fucking pervert?"

"Just a reminder that this is a communal space," Kyan yells, his tread getting heavier the further down the stairs he goes, "and I eat off that counter, so can you at least wipe it down after you're done having sex all over it?"

Zev shakes his head in annoyance. "Maybe this will teach you to start using the plates we bought, you fucking animal."

I hear a rustling, which I assume is Kyan grabbing his jacket off the coat rack. "I'm going to the office. Keep the fornicating behind your bedroom door from now on."

"Fuck you," Zev shouts just before the door slams shut.

I expect the moment to have passed. "I'm sorry," I say timidly as I pull my shirt down, but Zev stops my hand.

"Never," he says, his gaze piercing as it holds me, "ever be sorry. This is your house, and you are my mate. I'll pleasure you wherever the fuck I want." He pulls me to a seated position and gathers me in his arms as he lifts me off the kitchen island.

"Where to now?" I ask with a chuckle.

"My bedroom," he says. "I'm not letting Kyan ruin our first time together."

Our first time. Not only that, but Zev's first time ever. The importance of this is not lost on me as he kicks his door shut behind him and carries me over to the bed. "Are you sure?" I ask him. I know he wants this, but I want to make sure he understands that I'm his and there's no rush. "We can wait, if you'd feel more comfortable."

He pulls his shirt over his head in one fluid motion, and I suck in a breath at the sight of his shimmering blue abs and the black swirling tattoos that cover most of his chest and arms. "We can't wait," he replies. "I have waited centuries to find you, and I'm not wasting another second to make you mine."

"Centuries?" I ask, realizing I never considered that as an alien-dragon shifter, he might not be in his mid-thirties like me. "How old are you?"

He scrunches his nose as he thinks. "You lose track after a few centuries of life, but I'm pretty sure I'm early into my third century."

"Daaaamn, you're ancient," I say, giggling. I stroke a hand over his cheek. "You're very pretty for your age, old man."

Zev presses a kiss to my palm. "I thank you, wife." His lips move down to the pulse point on my wrist, and by the time they reach the crook of my elbow, I'm writhing on the bed like a cat in heat. We undress quickly, our hands desperate to find each other once more, and I gasp the second his pants fall to the floor.

Wrapping my hand around his cock, I mutter in awe, "You have ridges."

"I do. Only when I unmask."

"Then this is how I want you," I tell him. "Always."

He smiles, his different-colored eyes swirling with heat as he kisses my forehead. I inch backward on the bed and motion for him to follow. He grabs a condom from his nightstand and tears the packaging in half, and I have to close my mouth to keep from drooling at the way he slowly rolls it down the pulsing ridges of his long, spectacular dick. It barely fits him, but it'll do the trick.

"One kid is enough for me," I say, realizing we haven't addressed this yet. "I...I hope that's okay."

He crawls over me, settling himself at the apex of my thighs. "You and Nia are more than enough for me. You are everything."

I can tell by the way his hand trembles as he inserts a finger that he's nervous and probably wants to be certain I can take him, but I'm already soaking wet from our almost-hookup in the kitchen, and my body feels like it's buzzing with tension. "I'm ready," I say, reaching down and stroking his length. "I want you now."

He groans and pumps into my hand. Removing his finger, he lifts it to his mouth and sucks my come off so obscenely that I know I'm blushing. "Mm," he says, his tongue lapping up every drop. "I never want this taste to leave my skin."

I suck in a breath when he slowly enters me, his ridges brushing against my walls in an unexpected way, setting off my nerves like fireworks across the night sky. He's holding his breath, and his muscles are taut by the time our hips meet. Poor thing. Trying so hard to hold back for me.

"Let go," I tell him, wiping the sweat forming along his brow. My toes curl at the way he's stretching me, my walls fluttering around him and dying for more friction. "It's okay." I need more, anything more than just stillness, because that's making me want to scream.

His breaths are shallow and fast as he pulls almost all the way out, but at least he's breathing. It takes two hard thrusts before he roars into my neck as he comes, his body heavy as it collapses on top of me, spent and sated. He's still shaking, so I rub his back and revel in the comfort of his weight. He's almost like a weighted blanket.

And I don't mind that I didn't get the chance to come. It wasn't bad sex; it was just really fast. Zev's nothing if not generous though. Maybe I ask him to finish me off with his fingers?

Putting his weight on his forearms, he shifts back and pulls out. "One second," he says. Tossing the used condom in the little trashcan beside his bed, he reaches over and grabs another from his nightstand. I watch him carefully roll it over his ridges, then he gets back into place. "This will be better," he assures me.

I'm confused by his sense of urgency. I find it sweet, of course, but how can he be ready again so soon? "Are you sure?" I ask. "Don't you need some time to recover?"

He shakes his head. "My brothers have said the first time is always too quick," his mouth curves up into a wolfish grin, "but I'm not done with you yet, wife."

Pressing his swollen head through my folds, my nails bite into his back as he pushes all the way in.

"Ah!" I cry as he fills me.

He reaches a hand between our bodies as he pulls out, and surging forward, his thumb rubs against my clit, the pressure of it so divine that goosebumps race across my flesh, and my body begins to tremble.

My eyes remain pinched shut as Zev continues fucking me so hard that the headboard slams against the wall, and I don't open them again until I hear him say, "Yes, Charlie. My sweet, sweet Charlie." His gaze is locked on my breasts as they jump with each thrust. The sound of skin slapping together fills the air, so loud and rhythmic and hot.

He leans down and kisses me like he's running out of air and I'm the source. I've never been kissed like this. Like he owns me, but also cherishes me. I didn't think this kind of kiss existed. Then again, I didn't think someone like Zev existed either.

My clit aches to the point of pain and my walls clench tightly around him as he gets me closer and closer to release. "I need," I whimper against his lips. "I need…"

Zev sucks on my bottom lip, letting his teeth sink into it just enough to send a jolt of electricity up my spine. "I know," is all he says through ragged breaths before his thumb flicks and swipes my clit like he's been doing this for years. An expert on what my body needs.

I shatter mere moments later, letting fly an array of sounds and words I can't even understand as my body comes completely undone in his arms.

He follows me, throwing his head back with a guttural howl that could be heard two towns over. Shadows shift through the open window, creating a darkness around him that would scare me if I didn't trust him with my life. The wild state of his hair makes him look like a beast unhinged. My beast. My dragon. My mate.

Reluctantly, he pulls out and removes the condom before returning to the cradle of my arms. At some point, our bodies shift, and I end up on my side, with my head pressed against his chest. The steady beat of his heat lulls me to sleep.

CHAPTER 18

ZEV

The day of the hearing arrives, and Charlie is a nervous wreck. I stand by her side in the courtroom and answer the many questions the judge has about my occupation and net worth. The judge reviews the character statements from Charlie and Evan, and grills her on how she spends her time, her money, and why she's moved around so frequently since Nia was born.

My mate remains steadfast and confident as she answers each question, but she struggles with the latter. She tells the judge that she didn't feel safe around Evan, and only had her daughter's safety in mind when she chose to move to a different town and start her life anew.

Evan gets much easier questions to answer, and Charlie is noticeably annoyed by it. I am too, but I promised her I wouldn't electrocute the judge, so I'm doing my best to remain calm.

This man, if you can call him that, has the integrity of a bank robber and the spine of a jellyfish, yet the judge repeatedly thanks him after each question he answers as if he did the judge a personal favor. When Charlie answers a question, the judge stops listening halfway through.

Councilman Vincent makes an appearance, stating for the record that he's honored to have a man like Evan Campbell in politics, as,

"There are so many policymakers nowadays that you just can't rely on." Then he proceeds to tell the judge that the two of them have shared meals and beers in recent days, and that Evan's outlook on the state of the American family is uplifting. "He has the traditional values we need more of, frankly," Vincent adds.

Charlie rolls her eyes. I don't blame her.

When Officer Burton enters the courtroom, my teeth begin to grind, and I can feel the tension coming off Charlie in waves. He doesn't have much to say about Charlie, other than noting how her expired registration could be an example of neglectful parenting. Instead, he chooses to focus on me and my brothers, and how we seem to be involved in every major incident that has occurred in Sudbury as of late. His thin lips wobble when he starts talking about his late nephew, Trevor, and what an "upstanding citizen" he was, before his unfortunate and highly suspicious death.

"I'm not suggesting Mr. Monroe here was directly involved in my nephew's death, but his brother Axil and Axil's wife, Vanessa, made their hatred for Trevor quite clear."

None of this is relevant to Charlie's case, and I want to scream at the judge for allowing it to continue, which it does, with Burton's retelling of the drag time story hour that he busted up at the library, and how my brother Mylo clearly disregarded the concerns of members of the town who opposed the event. Then he says, his hand resting on his chest. "The only thing I want is for the people of Sudbury, and the children, especially, to remain safe from the evils that run amok in our society. Congressman Campbell shares my concerns, and in the short time I've gotten to know him, I can see that his only goal here is to give his daughter the care she deserves."

Sadly, it comes as no surprise that Evan is awarded visitation. The judge orders Charlie and Evan to work out a schedule where Nia can spend time with Evan in New Jersey, and the rest of the time with Charlie here in Sudbury. Charlie is distraught as I lead her out of the courtroom, but she tries to hide it from Evan. I rub her back and carefully plant myself so I block Evan from seeing her face. He wants to revel in her defeat, but I won't let him.

"This means he doesn't get to make any decisions about her care or education, right?" I remind Charlie. "And it's not shared custody, so she won't have to spend as much time with him."

"It doesn't matter," she says, her shoulders shaking as the tears fall. "I don't want him spending any time with her. Even a minute is enough to scar her for life."

"We won't let that happen," I vow.

She wipes her nose on the sleeve of her sweater. "What do you mean? There's nothing we can do."

Everyone is outside the courtroom waiting to hear the news. Her dad, my brothers, their wives, even Caitlyn. The women surround her in a tight circle, pushing me toward the back. I don't mind, especially when I see Charlie sagging against them. Together, they're holding her up, and that's precisely what she needs.

As a group, we make our way to the parking lot, and Darius pulls me aside. "Listen, Zev. I know y'all got together really quickly, and I'mma be honest, I was worried. It felt like she was rushing into something she wasn't ready for, especially with this Evan nonsense. I got caught up in my own regrets and that bastard almost swayed me. But now I see him for what he is, and you ain't him."

"I understand, sir," I tell him. "It took me by surprise as well, but I wouldn't change a thing."

His mouth quirks up on one side. "I believe you." He shoves his hands in his pockets, his car keys making a soft jingle. "I'm glad she has you. Her and Nia. They need something steady, you know? Someone they can count on."

"I do. I'll be whatever they need me to be."

He pats me on the back. "Good. That's what a father wants to hear." Then he makes his way to Charlie and wraps her in a tight hug, promising her that everything will be okay.

Nia is in school for another hour, so Charlie and I head home; our fingers entwined the entire ride. She's quiet and distant, and I don't blame her. Today was atrocious, and I'm not sure there's anything I can do to make it better.

That doesn't mean I'm not going to try. "I have a gift for you," I tell her once we get inside.

"Yeah?" she asks, her voice dejected as she flops face down onto our bed.

It's okay. I'll have her attention soon enough.

I pull my guitar from the closet and take a seat in my desk chair. Strumming it a few times, it awakens in my grip, ready to be played. Within the first few notes, Charlie's head lifts off the comforter. Clearing my throat, I start to sing.

"Oh my god," Charlie says after the first few lines, her eyes rimmed with tears as she sits up. Her hands cover her mouth as she listens. She mouths the words along with me but has to stop soon after she starts when the tears become a steady stream down her cheeks.

She doesn't let me finish the song. I get about halfway through "Iris" before she knocks the guitar out of my hands and jumps into my lap. Her lips roam my face, leaving light kisses on my cheeks, my nose, my eyelids, even my chin.

She sniffles as she pulls back to look at me. "You learned 'Iris?' For me?"

I nod. "It's your favorite song."

Her eyes flick back and forth between mine as she continues to cry. I wrap my arms around her, letting her know she's right where she belongs. "When?"

"After our first class."

She laughs. "I can't believe it took me this long to realize you had no business being in my class."

I hold my hands up, trying to look innocent. "The machines talk to me. I don't usually talk back. I just listen."

Charlie leans against me, her tears falling onto my cheek. "I love you."

"Not as much as I love you."

I lean in and take her lips. This kiss is not sweet or soft. Yearning drives us both as our tongues dance and our hands claw at each other. Lust thickens in my veins as she rolls her hips, my cock hardening, desperately seeking her wet heat.

She shifts in my lap and reaches for my belt. Her eyes remain locked on mine as she gets to her feet and unbuttons my pants. Charlie drops to her knees as she slides them down my thighs, my boxer briefs with them.

The moment she places me on her tongue, I let out a loud groan at the exquisite warmth. I have never felt such instant euphoria, and it takes the entirety of my strength to remain upright.

A breathy moan escapes her as she closes her plump lips around my head, my cock disappearing inside her mouth as she tries to take all of me. She fails, only getting about halfway down my length before I hit the back of her throat.

As soon as she hollows her cheeks and swirls her tongue against my ridges, my vision blurs, and I grip her hair tightly, pulling her back before I can spill into her mouth. I can't come yet. Her needs must be addressed before mine.

"Get naked for me," I tell her as my cock falls from her lips.

She doesn't comply. Not entirely. She removes her pants, underwear, and socks before crawling back into my lap. "No time for that," she pants, rolling her hips over my aching cock. "Need you now."

I can see in the swirling copper depths of her eyes that she's in pain and wants to forget it all. While I may not be able to erase that pain, I can give her what she wants. "Condom," I remind her before we get too carried away. She hops off me and grabs one from the nightstand and with shaking hands, tears into it and rolls it over my length as best she can. Human condoms were not made for males like me.

Charlie throws her head back with a moan when I push up into her, and my mind is gone the first time her walls clench around me. She feels so good, and my hands quake as I squeeze her perfect breasts through her shirt. They fit perfectly inside my palms, not spilling over, but just enough that I can cup and massage them. Her back arches as she pushes them deeper into my hands.

She grips the back of my chair as she lifts her hips and sinks back down, impaling herself on my cock. Keeping her small feet planted on the floor, she continues this, and I arch my hips to meet her, slamming into her velvety depths.

"More," she moans through gritted teeth.

If more is what she wants, that's what I'll give her.

As I continue to drive into her welcoming body, she lets out a keening cry. "My god! More, Zev. I need more."

I give her everything I have, the chair squeaking beneath us as if it might collapse into a pile of rubble.

She explodes around me, her entire body jerking in my arms as her walls flutter around me, sending me with her into the abyss of pure ecstasy. The world disappears apart from her face, and I focus on the love radiating in her deep brown eyes as I come. Jets of my seed fill the condom as my body weakens, and she sags in my arms.

Hauling her soft, supple body in my arms, I carry her to the bed and tuck her beneath the warm comforter. Removing my shirt, I climb in beside her, tucking my body around hers in a way that I hope will make her feel safe, in a time when she feels anything but.

Charlie awakens me an hour later by pressing soft kisses to my chest and tells me it's almost time for Nia's school day to come to an end. We dress quickly and pick up Nia from preschool, stopping for ice cream on the way home. Charlie doesn't want to tell her about Evan.

"Not today," she said. "Let today just be about us."

We order pizza for dinner, and let Nia pick the movie we watch. She chooses the live-action version of *The Little Mermaid* and screams the lyrics to every song. Charlie helps her get ready for bed, making sure she brushes her teeth and puts her bonnet on. I read her a story, and then another, and after the third, she starts nodding off, so I close the book quietly and back out of the room, flicking the light off as I go.

When Charlie and I climb into bed, she starts crying again; the protective bubble of our night as a family now faded. I hold her in my arms and rub her back, wishing there was something I could do to take her pain away.

The door to our room flies open, hitting the door stopper and letting out a loud *boiiing* that seems to go on forever. Nia giggles as she runs into the room and leaps onto the bed.

Charlie laughs as Nia wiggles her way between us.

"Baby," Charlie says, pretending to be annoyed by her presence. "What do you think you're doing in here?"

"I want to sleep in the big bed," she says, grabbing the remote and pressing all the buttons at once.

"Oh, you do?" I ask, tickling her tummy.

"And who said you can do that?" Charlie adds, nudging Nia's tiny body closer to me. "Both of y'all need to move over. How am I supposed to sleep like this?"

Nia rolls her eyes. "Baby girl, am I 'posed to care about this? 'Cuz I do not."

We're both so shocked by her attitude that we just start laughing.

I hold up my hand in surrender. "She wins. I'm not arguing with that."

Charlie and Nia fall asleep first, Nia's head pressed against Charlie's chest, and her leg thrown over my stomach. It's the least comfortable I've ever been in my own bed, but I don't dare move her. She's too cute to be disturbed.

I don't know how much later I wake up to Nia's screams. "What is it?" I shout, masking immediately as I leap to my feet.

"There's someone in the house," Charlie whispers, pulling Nia into her arms.

"Stay here," I tell them, marching toward the door, my draxilio eager for a fight. If Evan has entered my house, I'm fairly certain it's within my legal rights to melt the skin off his bones.

"Take a bat or something!" Charlie shouts.

"Why would I need a bat?" I call back. Then, lowering my voice so Nia can't hear, I add, "I can control every machine in the house."

I know before I make it down the hallway that it's Kyan, but he's not alone.

"Kyan," I growl, trying to identify the woman sitting at the counter. I've never seen her before. Her hair is black and straight and stops just above her collarbones. Her attire is far too formal for the setting and the time of day, though her aesthetic seems to match Kyan's. Uptight and lacking in flair. She's thick in the middle like Charlie and the rest of the women in our lives, and she appears to be of Chinese American descent. "What are you doing?"

He stumbles around the kitchen, tripping over his own feet, a steady giggle rumbling his chest. "Oh, heyyy, brother. You want some popcorn?"

I've never seen him like this. So...happy, and carefree. Is he drunk? High? Maybe both?

"No. You woke us up. You scared Nia."

"Nia?" the woman asks. "Who's Nia?"

"I'm Nia," she says from right behind me, making me jump. I had no idea she was even standing behind me.

"Ooh, it's a baby," the woman coos. She's clearly riding the same high Kyan is.

"And who the hell are you?" Charlie asks, glaring at her.

The woman waves. "Hi. I'm Naomi."

"This is Naomi," Kyan echoes. "She's my new assistant."

"I'm his new assistant."

"Okay," Charlie says, exasperated. "We get it." She looks at me with an *are you going to handle this?* expression, and I nod, my blood boiling at Kyan's utter disregard for what took place today.

Naomi doesn't seem to notice Charlie's tone and focuses on the light pink steel water bottle between her hands.

The moment Charlie and Nia close the door to our room behind them, I wrap my fingers around the collar of Kyan's perfectly pressed dress shirt and yank it toward me.

"Ahh f-, what the fuck?" he stammers once he regains his balance.

"Explain yourself," I demand. "You can't just stroll in here in the middle of the night with your assistant. High or drunk or whatever the hell you are."

"Why not?" he asks with an arrogant smirk. "I can do what I want. I live here too."

I've grown tired of his selfishness and lack of respect for everyone around him. "No, you can't. Do you know why?"

"Nope, why?"

"Because my wife and daughter live here now too, and they woke up terrified that someone was breaking into the house. Do you have any concept of what we've gone through today? Of what lies ahead?"

He throws his hands up. "I'm sorry that you had a bad day, but not everything revolves around you, you know? I had a bad day too," he says with a pout. He grabs a bottle of wine and rips the cork out. "Does anyone care?" He tips the bottle back and pours the contents down his throat. "Nope, nobody gives a fuck about Kyan because they're all too busy with their families and their jobs and their soon-to-be-born babies. And their foreign cousins!"

I don't know why he shouted that last part, but it's clearly a source of frustration for him.

As much as I want my brother to feel at ease, I can't allow this recklessness to continue. My duty is to Charlie and Nia. "Well, if this is how you choose to end a bad day, you need to do it somewhere else."

"Oh yeah? What are you saying?" he spits. "That I should move out?"

"Maybe you should."

He jerks back as if he's been slapped. "Wow." Taking another big swig from the bottle, he swallows and shakes his head. "Remember when it was just us? Me and you?"

I honestly don't. "What are you talking about?"

"Oh, come on. We got here, and the rest of them started pairing up, one by one. And who was left? Me and you."

"If this is about you not finding a mate—"

"I don't fucking want a mate!" he yells. "I never did. I came here because you all wanted to come here, and I didn't want to live without you."

He steps toward me, pressing the bottle into my chest, his teeth already stained red.

"You're acting like a child."

Lowering his voice, he continues, "And when we were on Sufoi, and the rest of them were taking down the king's enemies and you were getting punished by our handlers, who defended you? Me! It was you and me. It's always been you and me."

I don't know what to say to him. He did defend me against our handlers, which often resulted in him getting whipped right beside me. I didn't realize I owed him a debt for it though.

"I guess those days are over," he says, swinging the bottle at his side as he heads for the front door. "Come on, Naomi. We're leaving."

It takes her a second, but eventually she hops down from her stool and follows him out.

I go to bed feeling somewhat guilty that Kyan is so upset, but I don't regret letting him leave. As I wrap my arms around Charlie and Nia, I realize that my entire world is right here. There's nothing that will ever matter more.

CHAPTER 19

CHARLIE

"Maybe we should do this another day," I tell Zev as we hover outside Nia's room. The door is closed, and I can hear her humming softly as she plays.

He sighs as he rubs my back. "We have to do it eventually, and you've been putting it off for days. It's better to get it over with, right?"

I hate that he's right, but he's right. Knocking on the door, I say, "Can we come in, baby girl?"

"You may," she calls back in her sweetest tone.

My smile is tight as we enter and join her on the floor, and I hope she can't see right through it. Zev grabs Otto from Nia's bed and hands it to her. She takes it happily and gives Otto a tight squeeze. A simple thing that I wouldn't have thought to do but that will ensure her comfort throughout this conversation. That's why he's my mate.

"There's something we have to talk about," I begin. My hands are already shaking, so I tuck them under my thighs so she can't see. "You know that man who came to dinner? Evan?"

Her face hardens. "The suit man," she says, looking so exasperated by the mention of his name that you'd think he's as much her enemy as he is mine.

"Yeah, the suit man," I reply. "Well, baby…"

The words lodge in my throat. I need to tell her, but I don't want to. Putting them out into the air will only solidify the fact that this asshole is now a permanent part of our lives.

Zev grabs my hand and gives it a reassuring squeeze, and it helps me continue.

"Well, Evan is actually your biological father," I explain. "Five years ago, Evan and I made you." Christ, am I going to have to explain sex to her right now?

She looks between me and Zev, confused. "I thought Zev was my new daddy."

Zev smiles, and it breaks my heart, because he is, and he deserves to be, the only father figure in her life. "I love you, Nia," he says, touching her cheek. "It's an honor to be your dad, or whomever you want me to be." He places a hand over his heart. "I'll always be there for you. Evan's place in this family doesn't change who I am to you, and it never will."

Nia tilts her head. "So…I have two dads?" She holds up two fingers as her little brow furrows.

"No," I correct her, because this is an important distinction to make, especially if Evan is as terrible to her as I expect him to be. "Zev is your dad, and Evan is your father." I don't care if it seems petty. My daughter needs to know where her true home is. "And he wants to spend time with you. Get to know you better. As your father," I say, my teeth clenching, "that's his right."

"But it won't be that often," Zev adds, "and not for long stretches of time either. We just want you to get used to the idea of spending time with him."

"What if I don't want to?" she asks, her chin dipping as she strokes Otto's soft pink fur.

I just want to scream at the top of my lungs, "Then you don't have to and that settles that!" but that's not an option, unfortunately. When she gets older, her say in the matter will hold weight. For now though, we're stuck. "It might be weird at first to be around him and his family without me there," I tell her, patting Otto's head. "You can call me anytime, day or night, if you're feeling homesick, and we'll get through this together, okay?"

She nods and doesn't say anything else. After a few minutes, she starts talking to Otto and flying him around the room, and I wonder if she understands the talk we just had.

The fear of having to do it all over again, and knowing the day will soon come when I'll have to watch him drive away with her in the back seat sends hot tears to my eyes, and I scramble to get to my feet before Nia sees them fall.

Zev kisses Nia on the head before he follows me out, and I collapse into his arms the moment we're in our room.

The next few days pass in a blur of depression and anger as I trade emails with Evan's wife, Finley, regarding Nia's first visit to their home. Evan couldn't even be bothered to reach out himself to coordinate his daughter's arrival. Finley's emails are perfectly pleasant, but it's impossible not to hate her as much as I pity her. She's allowing this man to take my daughter from me—a daughter he doesn't even want to spend time with—without saying a peep. Her silence makes her complicit.

That's why I'm so glad Sam and Mylo's Halloween party is today. I get the entire afternoon to forget about Evan and Finley, and the fact that Nia has been court-ordered to spend time with her biological father when the best father she could ask for is right here, soaking up every minute he has with her.

I wouldn't be able to handle any of this without Zev. He's become my rock. Alien, dragon, whatever. He's more perfect than the majority of human men, and I'm just lucky enough that the fire-breathing beast inside him picked me.

"You ready?" Zev asks, looking at me in the reflection of his mirror. We decided to dress up as our three favorite things: Zev is a cheeseburger, I'm a large carton of french fries, and Nia is a milkshake. Our costumes are bulbous and oversized, but I'm comfortable, and I know everyone at the party will get a kick out of it.

We walk down the street, or waddle, rather, toward Sam and Mylo's new house, slowing as we climb the slight hill that their house sits atop. I'm out of breath by the time we arrive, but the speakers are blasting "Monster Mash," which instantly improves my mood.

Zev and I make our way through the crowd, which is mostly the brothers, their wives, Ryan, and Hudson and Cooper, Luka and Harper's teenage sons. Kyan is here, dressed in an oversized squirrel costume, sulking by the cooler. I steer clear of him. The vibe has been tense since Kyan and his assistant Naomi came home and caused a ruckus, and I don't think he and Zev are currently on speaking terms.

As for the rest of the costumes, everyone really turned out. Vanessa and Axil are dressed as Jim and pregnant Pam from *The Office*, Sam and Mylo came as a raven and Edgar Allan Poe, respectively, with Sam proudly sporting her new raven tattoo on the inside of her forearm that Zev did for her a few days ago. Luka, Harper, and their sons dressed up as red pins on Google Maps, which is particularly genius, and Ryan is sporting a Batman costume.

"This is what I wear every year," he told me. "It's timeless, and I look cute in it."

Sam throws her arm over my shoulder and plants a wet kiss on my cheek, no doubt leaving her black lipstick in a big smudge on my face. "I'm so glad you guys came."

"Ooh, you've had a few spiked cups of cider, haven't you?" I ask.

"Oh my god," she says with a gasp, removing her arm and planting herself in front of me. "Did I tell you about Burton pulling my brother over for speeding?"

"What? No," I reply. Not that I'm surprised. You'd think a cop at his level wouldn't be so horny for issuing tickets, but here we are.

"Yeah, he gave Marty a two-hundred-dollar ticket for that shit, and Marty was going three miles over the limit. Three."

"Wow," is all I can say.

Sam takes a big sip from her red cup and lets out a disapproving groan. "You know that anonymous tip line I set up at the newspaper? I've been getting dozens of emails from the same person about Burton. I don't know who it is, because it's like this weird Gmail account with mostly numbers in the name, but all the emails reference Burton's reign in the late nineties."

Well, now I'm intrigued.

"There are a bunch of people, maybe nine or ten, who Burton arrested for minor drug offenses, mostly weed, who went missing just weeks later," Sam explains. "Their bodies were eventually found in various places and in varying states of decay, but this person thinks Burton was involved in their deaths."

"Holy shit."

Sam nods. "My editor and I are going to look into it next week. Not sure how much we'll find or if this source is even credible, but we'll see."

What a creepy piece of shit that man is. Whether he's involved in those murders or not, I have no doubt he abused his power while making those arrests.

Mylo makes his way over to us and pulls Sam in for a passionate kiss, to the point where I feel weird just standing there watching, so I wander around until I find Caitlyn.

Her presence is a wonderful surprise, and she came as Sarah from *Hocus Pocus,* which is perfect because Sarah is famously the most DTF out of the trio.

"I didn't realize you made peace with the girls," I tell her as we grab Jell-O shots off the drink table next to the bobbing-for-apples station.

She nods as she sucks down her shot. "I get the sense it's a trial run, but it's cool. I'll get there." Then she nudges me with her elbow and gives me a conspiratorial look. "Has Councilman Vincent backed off with the book review?"

"He has actually," I say. "Mylo sent in the report a week ago and hasn't heard anything since."

Caitlyn giggles. "Love it."

Uh-oh. I sense blackmail afoot. "What did you do?"

She wiggles in a sort of dance-y way. "I have photos. Clear ones. Clear as fucking day."

"Oh, shit." She is so much more devious than I expected, but as long as she's on our side, I don't care what she does.

Even though I didn't ask, she proceeds to describe the photos in

HER ALIEN STUDENT | 157

detail, including poses, props, and even the many outfits Vincent modeled for her. "Yikes."

Then an idea hits me. "Caitlyn, would you be interested in running for office? Getting a seat on the council?" It would certainly help to have someone in a position of power who doesn't hate us, and Mylo said not long ago that he'd bankroll anyone I deemed suitable to run. Caitlyn would be a unique choice, for sure, but she understands the systemic racism running rampant here needs to stop, and I bet she's gathered enough dirt on the rest of the members of the council that they'd do her bidding.

"Yeah, I'd love a bigger office."

Okay, so her priorities might need a little tweaking, but it's a start. "Let's talk about that sometime soon."

"It's a date! Anyway," she says with a carefree shrug, "time to get sloppy and fall on a dick."

I laugh as she heads toward the drink table, then sidles up to Kyan. Good luck with that, girl.

The fun continues as the night goes on. The kids bob for apples, we all carve pumpkins, and when the drink table grows sparse, we clear it off and use it for a round of flip cup. My heart melts at the sight of Hudson and Cooper helping Nia carve a pumpkin. They sit on either side of her and patiently guide her hand as she carves. Her two little dragon cousins. Someday, she'll learn the truth about her family, and it's going to absolutely blow her mind.

"Do you hear that?" Luka calls out, then immediately turns down the music.

Sirens. Blaring police sirens, and they're getting louder.

I race over to the kids. "Boys, I need you to take Nia inside, okay? Stay inside until we tell you it's safe to come out." They don't question it; they just take her hands and tug her along until the door closes behind them. I want to go with them. I don't want any part of what's coming, but the people around me are my family now. There's no way I can leave them.

The cop cars skid to a halt in front of the house, four of them, and slowly, one by one, the girls step beside me, their husbands getting in front of us, forming a wall of monsters between the women and the real villains. Well, I can't speak for the rest of them, but one villain. Officer Burton.

Through their bodies, I can see that his car is up over the curb, his front left tire creating a deep groove in Sam and Mylo's freshly cut lawn.

"Hands up!" he shouts. "Everybody, get your hands up!"

"What is this about?" I hear Zev ask from the very front. His voice is calm and steady, which settles my nerves, but only for a second. If Burton has his gun drawn, there's no telling what he'll do.

"Zev Monroe, you're under arrest for the murder of Congressman Evan Campbell."

Murder? Evan was murdered?

"What?" Zev asks. "I have no idea what you're talking about. I've been here all night."

His hands must drop to his sides because I hear Burton bellow, "Get your hands up where I can see them."

"They're up!" Zev shouts back. "I'm holding them up!"

No, Zev. Don't lose your cool right now. Stay calm. I know bullets can't hurt him, or, rather, they can't kill him, but I don't want any shots fired tonight. We need to avoid that.

"Campbell's car was crushed by a tree at approximately six thirteen this evening. He was inside his car at the time," Burton says.

"A tree?" Luka yells. "He was crushed by a fucking tree, and you think my brother is to blame?"

"Don't, Luka," I hear Harper say in a stern voice. "Don't antagonize."

"It's bullshit," Axil grumbles.

Who cares if it's bullshit? I want to shout. Just do what they tell you to do.

It does seem like a strange set of circumstances though. The weather today has been mild. I didn't realize Evan was still in town, but clearly, he was. Still, where would he have been parked that a tree just fell on top of him?

The only thing I know for sure is that Zev didn't do it.

"I know nothing about Campbell's death, Officer," Zev says. "I've been here all night."

"Don't you fucking move!" Burton yells, and my heart stops beating. Time slows to a halt. I peek around Sam's shoulder as I watch Zev take a step toward Burton, and I hear a faint click as he pulls the trigger. But that's it.

Nothing happens. The bullet doesn't leave the gun. Then something occurs that makes absolutely no sense. Burton looks down the barrel of his own gun, his gaze narrowed in confusion. That's when it goes off.

Burton groans as his hand flies to his right shoulder, blood pouring through his fingers from the wound.

His men call out to him, seemingly as confused as I am about what he just did, and unsure if they should race to his side or keep their guns trained on Zev.

Burton staggers backward as the color fades from his cheeks, and he bumps into the back of his car before he falls to the ground.

His car must've been in neutral because it starts to move, the wheels turning as Burton tries desperately to crawl away. It's no use. The car rolls slowly over his body as the other officers rush over and try to yank him free by his arms. They're too late.

I hear the cracking of his spine as the car continues to roll—a sound I will never forget—his bones like gravel beneath the wheel as it crushes him to death. It feels like it takes hours for the car to slow to a complete stop, but eventually it does, and Burton's feet are the only visible part of his body.

The officers scramble to move the car, one climbing behind the wheel, the others attempting to lift the vehicle by the corners, but just as they finally put space between the wheels and Burton's lifeless form, a high-pitched shriek cuts through the air, making everyone stop and look to the sky.

A humongous red bird dives through the clouds, its body the size of a plane. No, not a bird. Definitely not a bird. A dragon by the name of Ronan.

Everyone—police, party guests, and neighbors—stands silently, gasping as they try to make sense of the mysterious creature above.

The first one to make a sound is Zev when he runs toward me and pulls me into his arms, choking on emotion as he crushes my head against the strong wall of his chest.

Things blur together after that. Statements are taken by the surviving officers and neighbors speak in hushed tones as they compare notes about "that thing in the sky." Caitlyn is visibly distraught and is the first one to leave.

Ambulances arrive, and we go inside as they begin trying to lift the car off Burton. A news alert to Sam's phone an hour later confirms his passing, her editor begging for details that the police still have not provided. She doesn't answer, and instead sits silently in the living room of her new home.

None of us are ready to talk about it, and we decide to call it a night shortly thereafter.

I don't sleep. Neither does Zev. Nia asks questions we can't even attempt to answer, and eventually gives up and passes out in the big bed with us.

The next day, I text my dad and ask him to come pick Nia up. He's heard the news but doesn't press for details. I tell him I'll explain later. He agrees and tells me he'll bring her back around lunch.

Everyone meets at our house, even Dante and Ronan. Mylo texted them and told them to come.

When the two European dragons arrive, they stroll in with a bottle of champagne and balloons. Ronan doesn't look pleased to be wearing a sparkly blue party hat with gold tassels, but Dante is ready to rock. He pops the bottle, and it sprays all over the entryway as he dances in a little circle. He realizes he's alone in his celebration a beat too late and looks at us like a bunch of party poopers.

"What is wrong with you people?" he demands. "Your foes have been vanquished. You should be happy."

"Dante," Mylo says in a tone of clear warning, getting to his feet. "What have you done?"

"Other than give the town of Sudbury a complimentary flyover," Kyan barks out. "You've exposed us to our neighbors. Now we have to move!"

Dante puts the half-empty bottle of champagne on the coffee table. "You tell me there is an evil man who wants to steal your children," he begins, "so what do I do? I kill him. Drop a tree on his tiny car."

"Wait," Zev says, his tone filled with rage. "Who told you that? About Evan."

Mylo scrubs a hand down his face. "Dante, I told you those things in confidence."

"*You* fucking did this?" Kyan shouts at Mylo.

Mylo's face turns bright red as he faces us. "I met them at a bar near their Airbnb. We had a few drinks, and I told them about us. All of us. I don't know, that part just sort of slipped out."

"Jesus Christ," Vanessa mutters wearily.

Dante scoffs, his mouth hanging open. "I expected a thank-you. This is family, is it not? I protect you; you protect me."

Kyan seems elated at the resentment directed at Dante, but still bristling with rage. "And what about the flyover? In what world was that a good idea?"

Ronan clears his throat. "Now you have full cover," he says in a bored tone.

"Explain that one," Mylo says.

Sam nods in agreement. "Yeah, I don't get it."

"You are not red dragons, *aye*?" Ronan replies. "You are blue dragons. No one in your town is looking for a blue dragon. They are not even sure what they saw was a dragon. Some may have photos or videos. They will be blurry at best."

"And...what?" Axil mutters.

"This will become the talk of the town," Dante says, his cheery tone really getting under my skin. "Like in Siena," he says. "They see a dragon cut through the sky; they create entire *contrade* to honor it."

"You're saying this will become, like, Sudbury's mascot?" I offer, still not following how their actions will benefit us.

"Exactly!"

"There will be meals and restaurants and parades dedicated to the Red Dragon of Sudbury," Ronan says. "The interest in dragons will grow over time. It will start with rumors, then it will spread to artwork, then to merchandise."

"When your community honors what you are, they no longer fear you," Dante adds. "If there comes a day when you are spotted darting across the sky or shifting into your true form, your people will protect you, especially if you protect them in return."

"How long is that supposed to take?" Kyan barks. "A century? We don't have a century to see if our neighbors will keep our identities a secret."

Dante puts a finger to his mouth, shushing Kyan. And Kyan does not like that at all.

He gets in Dante's space, their chests puffed out and practically touching. "Get the fuck out of my house."

Dante looks around at us like we're his unruly children, but he doesn't seem mad, just disappointed. "So ungrateful." He grabs his bottle off the coffee table and heads for the door. "Come along, Ronan. Let us go home."

Ronan doesn't offer us a second look as he leaves, slamming the door behind him.

Hudson looks at his parents. "Are they really our cousins?" he asks.

"No," Luka replies, disgusted. "They are like us, but not. Not at all."

Zev shoots to his feet, causing all of us to jump. "I made the bullet stick," he admits. Then he turns to me, his gaze swirling with shame and regret. "I held it inside the barrel, and when he looked down, I let it go. I'm so sorry."

Hudson stands up next. "I made Burton look down the barrel."

Harper gasps and grabs her eldest son by the collar. "You did what?"

"Ma, stop." He pulls away, fixing his shirt. "I was watching from the window while Cooper read Nia a book, and I felt Burton's brain, mushy, just like you described, Dad."

Luka jerks back. "Don't bring me into this. I've never gone inside Burton's mind."

"Yes, you did," Vanessa points out. "When we broke Axil out of jail. Remember?"

"Shit," he says to himself. "I did, didn't I?" Then he turns to his son. "Well, I never told you to do that. I didn't even know you *could* do that."

"I noticed it about a year ago," Hudson admits. "You brought me with you to the DMV. That place was full of mushy brains."

"Good for you, buddy," Kyan says, giving his nephew's arm a squeeze.

"No, no, no." Luka shakes his head, wagging his finger at Kyan. "Don't encourage this."

"Why not? He defended his family against a terrible man. You should be proud of him." Kyan looks at Hudson. "You ever want to use those powers to change the world, come shadow me at the office."

Mylo starts laughing. "And what would shadowing you entail, brother? Shredding classified documents as you look down upon the peasants crossing the sidewalk in the shadows of your massive tower?"

"Fuck off, book boy."

"My son is not going to shadow you," Luka tells Kyan, but Hudson's gaze is filled with longing and something else as he looks at his uncle.

"Wait," I interrupt, a thought popping into my head that I can't shake. "Who moved the car? Did that happen on its own?"

"Uh, no," Vanessa says, meekly raising her hand. "That was me, I think."

Axil shakes his head as if he didn't want Vanessa to admit that.

Sam sucks in a breath. "What do you mean, *you think?*"

Vanessa straightens in her seat. "Well, um, remember when Harper showed us she can kind of breathe fire?" The rest of the group nods, but I certainly wasn't present for that. "I noticed last month that I could move things with my mind. It took a lot of practice. I started with a pencil, then a pepper shaker, then a baseball hat."

"Ugh, that's so much cooler than mine," Harper groans, dropping her chin to her clutched fist.

"When Burton's gun went off and he started to fall," Vanessa continues, "I focused on the front seat, and soon it was like I could see inside the car. It was in park, but I shifted it into neutral and let gravity do the rest."

It takes a moment to sink in, but when it hits, my bottom lip trembles. Every member of my family, my village, played a part in protecting me and my daughter. Even our European "cousins," though I still don't know if they're good or evil.

I suppose this discussion of morality will continue, especially if Hudson chooses to take Kyan up on his offer. The only thing I know for sure is that there's no other wall I'd rather stand behind, and no other monsters I want by my side in the days to come.

EPILOGUE

CHARLIE

TWO WEEKS LATER...

"*N*ia, let's go, baby!" I shout from outside her room. "We don't want to be late."

"Coming, Mommy," she replies, swinging open her door and trotting out in her new dress, Otto in hand. "Do I call Grandpa's girlfriend Grandma Joyce? Or Auntie Joyce?"

"Maybe ask her first," I tell her. "Some ladies don't like *grandma*. It reveals their age."

Nia looks up at me, biting her lip. "But Joyce looks like a grandma."

"Ooh, don't tell her that."

We're going to Dad's house for dinner after we swing by Sam and Mylo's to drop off some snickerdoodle cookies I made. Sam's been craving them, and I promised I'd make her a batch.

After Evan's passing, the custody fight fell apart, and sole custody is now mine.

I feel for Finley, having to raise a baby alone, but there has to be some part of her that's relieved he's gone. It's certainly how I feel. No more looking over my shoulder. No more living in fear that he'll show up out of the blue. Nia belongs to me and Zev, and that will never change.

It's also been nice driving around Sudbury without worrying about Officer Burton and how he'll terrorize us next. He was mourned by his fellow officers and members of the town after his death, but the period of mourning was over sooner than I expected.

His brethren in blue, local hunters, and other gun enthusiasts were quick to point out that the primary rule of gun safety is to keep the gun pointed away from you, and since he didn't do that, "Perhaps his mind was starting to go, and he kept his job longer than he should have." They seemed embarrassed for him, that he went out in such a blatant display of incompetence.

There's something particularly poetic about how he based his entire personality around his role as a power-hungry cop, and *this* is how he'll be remembered—a feeble old man who couldn't follow basic safety protocols.

With our two biggest threats now gone, life with Zev has gotten a lot easier. Zev has started filling out adoption paperwork for Nia, which sets my soul at ease, knowing we'll officially be a family in the days to come.

We're turning my bedroom, that I never really used, into a studio. He's most excited about making instrumental covers of the songs we love and maybe uploading them to Spotify. I keep telling Zev he needs to use that velvety voice of his and start singing, but he refuses. "I sing for you, but no one else," he told me. I'm not mad at it. I get that sexy croon all to myself.

Nia has started calling him "Dev," a combination of Dad and Zev. She tried "Zad," at first, but I put a real quick stop to that when I realized it was the shortened version of "Zaddy."

In turn, Zev has started calling Nia, "Nev." It doesn't make sense the way Dev does, but it's cute when they start addressing each other "Dev" and "Nev" while chasing each other around the kitchen counter.

And I, unfortunately, have become "Chev," which is a nickname I despise, but the two of them get so much joy out of it that I let it continue. Chev, Dev, and Nev—your neighborhood modern family. This is the new normal, I suppose.

I can't stay mad at them for long. Not even for a minute, really. I know because I've timed it. They're just too perfect. My brilliant, beautiful daughter, and my sexy-as-fuck alien husband.

We pull into Sam and Mylo's driveway, and Sam comes running out wearing a star headband and a necklace made of miniature Christmas lights. "Cookieeees," she growls with her mouth open, and her arms outstretched.

"Cool your jets, you monster," I say jokingly as I hand her the tin. "Christmas decorations already? It's not even Thanksgiving yet."

"So?" she asks as we follow her into the house. "The moment Halloween ends, I rip down the skeletons and start blasting Mariah."

"Good god," Zev grumbles, his hands covering his ears. The carols really are blasting when we get inside. Mylo comes out of the kitchen wearing a Christmas sweater and, even more appropriately, noise-canceling headphones.

He rolls his eyes and points to the headphones after placing a box of ornaments next to the naked tree.

"Can you turn that down?" I beg Sam. I don't have heightened senses like the boys, and even I can't take it.

"Fine, fine." She takes Nia by the hand and disappears into the kitchen with the cookies.

Vanessa sits on their recliner with her feet up, and waves happily once she sees us. "Guys, guys, check this out." She takes a second to make sure Nia is completely out of sight before focusing on the box of tinsel.

We stop in our tracks to watch her. Narrowing her gaze, she lifts a handful of tinsel from the box on the coffee table, and it glides across the room before it's tossed into the air, landing in even strands on the branches.

"Vanilla," Sam groans from the kitchen. "The tinsel goes on last. Can you save your party trick for later?"

"You're just jealous," Vanessa calls out.

"You're right," Sam hollers back. "I am."

"I don't have a dragon power," Axil says with a pout.

Mylo removes his headphones. "Hey, neither do I."

That is odd. I know Zev, Luka, and Kyan discovered theirs not long after they landed here. "Maybe yours haven't shown up yet either," I offer. "Give it time."

I wonder what mine will be. If I get one. Ooh, I hope it's a cloak of invisibility or something.

"Wait," Sam interjects, "what's Kyan's power? I just realized I've never seen it."

Axil chuckles low, shaking his head. "Yes, you have. It's anger."

Sam's brow furrows. "Anger? That's not a power."

Mylo blows out a breath. "It is the way Kyan wields it. You've seen glimpses of it, but never his full power. That's not something you want to see, trust me. His rage, when he really turns it on, could decimate an entire city with a single stomp of his foot."

Yeah, I don't want to be anywhere near him when that happens.

"Okay, well, we have dinner plans with Darius and Joyce," Zev says, heading into the kitchen to get Nia. "So we should get going."

We say our goodbyes and head for the door, but someone knocks just before I touch the knob.

On the doorstep stands a short, slim woman with blonde hair, a lip ring, smudged black eyeliner, and a flannel shirt that's three sizes too big. She looks at me, then slowly examines everyone behind me in a way that feels intrusive.

"Can I help you?" I ask.

"Kyan," she says, "Have you seen?"

Her accent is extremely thick, and I can't place it.

"Um, no. Sorry," I tell her. "We haven't seen him."

Kyan moved out a few days after the Halloween party. We don't know where he's staying. With his long work hours, he was barely at the house to begin with. I don't think any of the brothers have spoken to him.

"None of you have seen?" she asks, poking her head inside the door.

Luka steps forward. "I spoke to him last week, but I haven't heard from him since then. Why?"

Harper gasps. "Wait, you haven't talked to him in a week? What do you mean?"

"I mean, I haven't talked to him in a week," Luka repeats.

The woman puts her phone to her ear, and I hear her say, "Code Key. Code Key."

"Honey," Harper says, her voice raising an octave. "Hudson said he was going to shadow him today. I thought things were fine. Hudson said you told him it was okay."

"No!" Luka shouts. "I never said that."

"Excuse me," I say, tapping on the girl's shoulder. "What does Code Key mean?"

"Kyan is boss. He checks in every day. We have been told if he does not check in, he has been taken."

Harper pushes her way past us, leaning heavily on her cane. "What the hell do you mean *taken*? My son went to his office today to shadow him."

"If he was with Kyan, he taken too."

Luka makes his way to Harper's side. "You're saying my brother *and* my son have been taken?

Something about this is off. Well, everything about this is off.

"What exactly do you do for Kyan?" I ask, poking my head around Luka's arm.

She points to her chest. "Doctor."

"*You* are a doctor?" Sam asks. "Why are you dressed like a Hot Topic employee?"

"I forgot coat at lab." The doctor's phone buzzes in her hand. She holds up a finger. "Stay here. We find him."

"*You* are going to find him?" Luka asks skeptically. "No fucking way. My son is with him. I'm going to find him."

The rest of us exchange a knowing glance. I call my father and ask him if Nia can stay the night. Zev agrees to drive her over. When he returns, the rest of us are gathered in the living room, Kyan's doctor friend long gone. My husband cracks his knuckles, practically bouncing on his feet.

"Okay, let's go dragon hunting."

Just another night in Sudbury.

* * *

Thank you for reading HER ALIEN STUDENT! I hope you loved Zev and Charlie's story. Are you wondering what happened to Kyan? And who kidnapped him and Luka's son? Good news! You're about to find out!

Preorder HER ALIEN BOSS now!

ALSO FROM IVY

ALIENS OF OLUURA

Saving His Mate

Charming His Mate

Stealing His Mate

Keeping His Mate

Healing His Mate

Enchanting Her Mate

(This series isn't finished. There's plenty more to come!)

STRANDED ON EARTH

Her Alien Bodyguard

Her Alien Neighbor

Her Alien Librarian

Her Alien Student

Her Alien Boss (Coming April 2024)

ENJOY THIS BOOK?

Did you enjoy this book? If so, please leave a review! It helps others find my work.

Get all the deets on new releases, bonus chapters, teasers, and giveaways by signing up for my newsletter.

FROM IVY

J'll be honest, I was terrified to write a single parent romance. As much as I love reading them, as a childfree lady, I have no frame of reference when it comes to writing a child into creation. I spent hours on YouTube watching videos of five-year-olds, just to get a sense of how they act and think at that age. So first and foremost, I hope you enjoyed Nia and her many adorable moments, because that's what I worried about most with this story.

Zev and Charlie, on the other hand, arrived fully formed in my mind. Sending songs over text or DM seemed like a natural way for them to get to know each other, and I adored coming up with which songs would perfectly capture their day-to-day moods.

When Zev first shows up in *Her Alien Bodyguard*, he's tragic and tortured and has no sense of who he's supposed to be. Fast forward sixteen years, and he still has no idea. That was the most realistic part of him to me. It takes some of us decades to figure out who we are, and for Zev, the key to his sense of self was music. The moment he starts playing an instrument, he can sink into the sounds he's creating and forget the world.

Charlie has a much better idea of who she is going into this story, but as is the case with my other heroines of this series, and women in the real world, she's been dealt a crappy hand. Systemic injustice lurks around every corner, and she does her best just to get by. Despite the trauma she's still processing, her heart remains surprisingly open. That's my favorite thing about her. Even though she tries to manage it all on her own, she does end up leaning on others for support. She forms her own opinion of Caitlyn, despite the stories Sam and Vanessa have told her, and Zev's awkward comments don't scare her away. When most would give him an excuse and bolt, Charlie stays and asks more questions. Just that additional sliver of patience is life-altering for him, and it's something he doesn't expect.

Now, let's discuss the villains and their spectacular deaths, shall we?

I wasn't sure how I was going to kill off Evan Campbell at first. I just knew it would be off page, sending Burton and his cronies to the Halloween party to accuse Zev of murder. Dante dropping a tree on Evan's car was a great way to bring Dante and Ronan back into the fold, and it was also just hilarious to me. I actually giggled as I wrote it. He sees himself as this powerful figure in the world of American politics, only to die alone in his car in the middle of a town he thinks is a shithole.

You might've been surprised by Burton's demise, especially with one book in the series still to go, and I get that. Who's going to be the bad guy in the final book if Burton's dead? Well, when there are bad apples at the top, there's usually an underlying rot spreading through the orchard, and that's what you'll discover in Kyan's book. There are much darker forces at play in Sudbury, and it's time for them to step into the light.

You'll also learn wtf Kyan actually does for a living too, which I realize has been a long tease. I promise it's worth the wait. Our angriest Monroe brother has his hands tied in Her Alien Boss, and there's only one person who can help him out of it...his mysterious new assistant, Naomi.

You are going to LOVE her.

Stay tuned for the epic final installment of Stranded on Earth, coming to you April 2024!

Love,
Ivy

P.S. - A huge thank-you to my sensitivity reader, Grace. I loved getting to work with you again, and I'm so thankful for your insight into Charlie's life and mind.

P.P.S. - The early drafts of my books are messy piles of chaos, and it's only with the help of Tina, Mel, Chrisandra, and Jenny that they turn into beautiful book butterflies. These four angels polish my words and calm my fears, and I'm just an aimless scribbler without them.

RESOURCES

In Our Own Voice:
Black Women's Reproductive Justice Agenda
202.545.7660
blackrj.org

National Domestic Violence Hotline
1.800.799.SAFE (7233)
thehotline.org

SAMHSA (Substance Abuse and Mental Health Services
Administration Hotline)
1-800-662-HELP (4357)
TTY: 1-800-487-4889
samhsa.gov

RAINN (Rape, Abuse, & Incest National Network)
1-800-656-4673 (call or chat)
rainn.org

National Suicide Prevention Hotline
1-800-273-8255 (call or chat)
suicideprevention.org

ABOUT THE AUTHOR

Ivy Knox has always been a voracious reader of romance novels, but quickly found her home in sci-fi romance because life on Earth can be kind of a drag. When she's not lost on faraway worlds created by her favorite authors, she's creating her own.

Ivy lives with her husband and two neurotic (but very cute) dogs in the Midwest. When she's not reading or writing, she's probably watching *Our Flag Means Death*, *Bridgerton*, *The Fall of the House of Usher*, or *What We Do in the Shadows* for the millionth time.

Printed in Great Britain
by Amazon

45710880R00101